Matthew John was born in the unpronounceable town of Llanelli in South Wales in 1973. He began writing as soon as he left school. Unfortunately, due to chronic laziness and apathy, he didn't take anything seriously until the age of twenty-five, when, to his great surprise, he actually achieved something. Inspired by this, he bought a new pen and in six months wrote more than he had in the previous seven years.

Since then he has tried to write continuously, not leaving the house except in the direst circumstances, battling bravely against hangovers and nightmares about zombies. At present he lives invisibly in Carmarthen with his childhood sweetheart, to whom he owes everything.

ZOMBIE! ZOMBIE!

Matthew John

Zombie! Zombie!

Vanguard Press

A CIP catalogue record for this title is
available from the British Library
ISBN 1 903489 82 2

Vanguard Press is an imprint of
Pegasus Elliot MacKenzie Publishers Ltd.
www.pegasuspublishers.com

First Published in 2002

Vanguard Press
Sheraton House Castle Park
Cambridge England

Printed & Bound in Great Britain

Dedication

'For Sian
who divides my destination
and who thought of the basement.'

Chapter 1

The sky was a blue diamond and the air had never tasted so sweet. The five of us ripped up the road, weaving through the cars like noisy ghosts, on the way back to the City after another day's work. Cassie sat behind me with her hands wrapped around my stomach, pricking me with her fingernails. Every now and then she'd bite the back of my neck or put her mouth to my ear, telling me things that made me shiver. This was a special day; I was on ninety-eight, only two more to go. Six ahead of Laura, ten ahead of Kyle. He was three in front of Mina. Cassie didn't keep count, she said it spoiled all the fun.

We twisted the bikes through a few more cars before I spotted some movement. I pulled on the brake and skidded to a stop, the others falling into line behind. After stepping off the bike I took the sword from Cassie, the blade singing from its scabbard. The two zeds had been flowing along the side of the road, checking the cars for meat, but since they'd heard us they had turned and were advancing in that slow but remorseless way that all zeds have. I went to meet them, past one car, stopping before I met any blind spots. The zeds were close now, gurgling with eagerness. A man and a woman. He was middle-aged, paunchy, wearing what had once been a good suit and a single ruined shoe. She was a lot younger, dark haired, red dress, not in bad condition considering. She wasn't pure, though; ugly wounds marred both her arms and chunks of flesh had been torn from her neck.

The adrenaline began to pump as I waited, sword on high. The male zed took another step, the blade slashed and the zed's insides began spilling to the floor. "Gross out!" yelled Mina as the zed wailed and reached for me. I took another swipe and the zed's head rolled like a bowling ball across the windscreen of a car. The body thumped onto the road and started to twitch.

The other zed hesitated, growling. I took the opportunity and slashed open the front of her dress, jumping back to avoid her clutching hand. The zed was confused, actually trying to keep the front of her dress closed as she advanced, giving us glimpses of her red underwear. Her skin had that zed glow about it, like it was filled with moonlight, right here under the summer sun. The zed was looking at me now, a hundred types of hunger in her eyes. She came for me again, both hands this time, face twisted in a vacant snarl. I cut off her head and reached one hundred.

When I turned back I found Cassie cutting huge lines of celebratory whizz on the front of a car. The whizz was pure as the driven snow, cooked up by our chemist, Chloe, who had a lab up in the attic. Whizz kept us sharp. It froze the nerve steady and held the aim true, filling us with the fire we needed to deal with the zeds. We'd tried all the other drugs we could get our hands on but they'd made us too happy, too hooked, or too paranoid. We couldn't afford to be any of those things in our new zed world.

I put the sword into its scabbard and took a note from my pocket, rolling it for the only thing cash was good for anymore. I used the note to do two of the monster lines then I staggered back, looking around us. The motorway was clogged with traffic. The countryside around us had grown wild. All was still. The silence was something you couldn't believe, it made the eardrums bulge, searching for sound, hunting it out. And there was nothing, not out here anyway. In the City it was different.

Cassie was moving towards me with spots of powder

on her nose. She smiled as we stepped into each other's arms. Her hair was freshly dyed, copper, red and blonde. As we kissed I could taste bubblegum and whizz at the back of her throat. I put my hands on her ass and Cassie bit my tongue. Kyle was watching us with a wide grin on his face, a hand planted on Laura's shoulder. When Mina finished her lines we jumped back on the bikes and set off again towards the City, breakneck speed, dodging the cars, whizzing and laughing with not a care in the zed world.

The house we'd found was a beauty. It lay on the outskirts of the City, obscured by trees, the gardens surrounded by a high stone wall. The only way in was through the front gate which needed a remote to open it. Whoever had lived here before us had been as paranoid as hell. The house itself was long and low with the lab in the attic and a handy basement underneath. There was plenty of room for all of us. Myself and Cassie, Laura and Kyle, Mina, Chloe the chemist, and Bradley. He was the fixer in our group, the one who'd got the generators started. Bradley was a weird bastard though, and no one really felt comfortable with him. He just didn't fit in.

Bradley liked being alone for a start. I could never understand that. Whenever I was alone I'd just start thinking about all the zeds out there and I'd end up climbing the walls. The others were the same, except for Bradley. I think he actually kind of *liked* the zeds, if that was possible. He enjoyed going out into the City at night, alone, which was insane. You could never go *anywhere* on your own, but he did, coming back at dawn with a bizarre look in his eye. Sometimes he brought guns. Shotguns, machine guns, pistols. We had a major armoury thanks to Bradley.

That night five of us sat around the living room.

Bradley was in his library, Cassie down in the basement. Laura and Kyle lay on one of the couches, kissing noisily. I sat watching an old horror movie with Mina as Chloe cut more lines out on the coffee table. She had an insatiable appetite for whizz, it was like she was making up for Bradley's refusal to take any drug whatsoever, even coffee. Chloe was stick thin of course, and the tallest of the girls. She wore her brown hair in a smart bob and her scrawniness made her nose sharp and her mouth too wide. She snorted her lines and smiled to herself, taking a delicate sip of gin and tonic. As the movie was finishing Cassie came back looking breathless. She kissed me with cold lips then took the lines that Chloe was offering.

"Did you have a nice time?" Mina asked Cassie with what I thought was a naughty smile.

"I always have a nice time," said Cassie, taking a drink and dropping on the couch next to Mina. "So how shall we celebrate?"

"Celebrate what?" asked Chloe, putting a disc on the stereo that had once been worth a huge amount of money.

"Alex's hundred," said Laura, climbing off Kyle and stretching. She turned to me. "What does Alex want to do?"

"Just to have a good time," I said, meaning it. What else could you do when the world was full of zeds?

Since the streetlights had gone out the view from the balcony at night was wondrous, as long as the clouds stayed away. The sky was an inky majesty of twinkles. When you looked at it the zeds didn't seem like such a problem after all. I was standing there with Cassie and Mina, breathing in the night, waiting for the downers to kick in. With all the whizz around they were the only things that could make us sleep, and they helped control the nightmares. I listened hard and heard something, so

14

faint that it could have been my imagination, although I knew that it wasn't. A multitude of moans carried on the breeze, a distant wail from the City. The fucking zeds were a problem all right. Mina had started to cry so we took her through the lab and downstairs to our bedroom. We undressed then stripped Mina, switching off the light and climbing into bed with Mina shivering between us. I kissed her while Cassie held her tight, whispering comforting things, making her feel better, until the pills came on and put us to sleep.

We ate breakfast in the afternoon followed by the countless vitamin pills that Chloe asked us to take. It was a glorious day, the sunlight streaming through the kitchen, making things look weirdly normal and everyday. Bradley shattered the illusion by stomping into the kitchen with a .45 in his hand. "Aren't you ready yet?" he asked irritably.

We all turned to him in confusion. "Ready for what?" said Mina.

"Haven't you looked in the fridge's recently? Food and water are running low. It's time to go shopping." Shopping was a big thing, an adventure. It was the only activity that we all had to do together. It made us an unit, a team. We put our lives in each other's hands. I was ready to go, excitement building. Bradley slapped a list onto the table. "We leave in an hour," he said.

A shopping expedition called for huge amounts of whizz to sharpen us up and keep us all brave. Chloe cut piles of the stuff onto the kitchen table and as she sorted it out into lines I went to wake up Cassie. She tried pulling me into bed until I explained what was going on. After that she rolled off the mattress and followed me into the kitchen, rubbing her eyes. Within half an hour we'd all had our lines, except for Bradley of course, and it was time to tool up in the armoury.

"I'm having the shotgun."

"Kyle, you had it last time."

"No fucking way. You had it last time."

"No, it was you. Remember shooting that zed's foot off?"

"That's right! It tried to hop and fell on its ass."

"Yes, so I'm having the shotgun."

"I'll take this then. What is this, Bradley?"

"It's an SA80, modified by Heckler and Koch."

"Pass me the Uzi."

"Shit, I'm going to sneeze."

"Clear it out with this."

"Fuck off! Don't point that thing at me!"

"Everybody calm down, there's plenty for us all. Cassie and I get the carbines. Laura can take the shotgun, Kyle and Chloe get the SA80s. Alex and Mina take the Uzis. All right? Good. Now then children, make sure you're all carrying sidearms in case you run out of ammunition or your weapons jam, and remember the cardinal rule; always stick together, always go for the headshot. Are we ready?"

Shopping in one of the superstores would have been impossible. We always hit the supermarkets, it was easier to deal with the zeds that way. Chloe was our driver, this time Cassie rode shotgun. The two of them were going to wait in the car park, picking off stray zeds. The rest of us would take a trolley and go inside. Water was number one on our list, the supply always had to be kept high. We also needed alcohol, cans and dried goods. The food we had to eat was rarely too high in the taste stakes but no one seemed to mind. Last on the list were cigarettes and lighters, added by Laura when Bradley hadn't been looking.

We loaded the guns into the back and climbed inside the huge jeep. The whizz was hitting hard and confidence was high. Cassie hit the remote to open the gates, Chloe rolled us down the driveway and we were on the road. We didn't see any zeds on our street but that didn't mean there weren't any around. We drove out of Hemdale Gardens, the roads pretty clear. The only ones that were clogged led to and from the City centre. It took about thirty minutes to reach the supermarket. After ten we saw our first zed of the day. It was weaving along the pavement in a world of its own but when it heard the jeep it stopped and raised its messy head. Kyle opened the window to wave at it as we drove past and Mina laughed. I looked back and saw the zed turn to follow us down the road.

Chloe made a right at the supermarket, then another right into the car park. Fifteen or more zeds began closing in and others would soon be on their way. We grabbed the guns from the back and leapt outside, flying on the whizz now, eager for the fray. We formed a quick circle around the jeep and started shooting, taking our time, aiming carefully between the zeds' eyes. They began to drop, some of them crawling or getting back up again, most of them staying down. It took about two minutes to clear the car park and when we'd stopped firing there were nearly thirty zeds on the ground, heads blown open, skin already beginning to lose that captivating shine.

It was time to move. I kissed Cassie goodbye and took a trolley from the rusting pile. Bradley was in front of me, rifle stuck to his shoulder. Kyle stood on my left, Mina to my right. Laura was at the back. We made our way through the open doors and waited, letting our eyes grow accustomed to the darkness. We heard the crack of a rifle behind us, Cassie dropping another zed. The supermarket seemed deserted, the tills raided, goods scattered over the floor. Bradley slowly led the way into the aisles.

"Where the fuck are they?" said Kyle, waving the machine-gun.

"Just stay alert," Bradley whispered. The wheels of the trolley were squeaking on the floor. Something moved up ahead. Bradley shot it and a zed slumped to the ground. A thick moan sounded from somewhere on the left. We carried on up the aisle, tension building. "The water's at the top," Bradley told us. "Be careful when we get there." There was more shooting outside, six reports. The nerves were beginning to get to me, it felt like we were moving much too slowly. If it was up to me we'd have run in blasting, but we'd learned that it was usually best to do things Bradley's way.

He hopped out at the top of the aisle and immediately began shooting. Kyle joined him, Laura called out, I turned and saw three messy zeds moving up behind us. Laura and Mina put them down, Mina cackling with whizz-fuelled glee. I loaded the trolley with the biggest bottles of water, deafened by the gunfire. Bradley dropped another zed and it was time to move on. The next aisle was full of alcohol. We stepped carefully over the bodies, making sure not to slip on the blood, then took down bottles of whisky, gin, wine and vodka. Laura blew a zed's head off when it popped up behind one of the tills, breaking some tension and making us laugh. We moved through more aisles, collecting packets and cans. Another shot rang out from the car park. Now there was only one more aisle to go.

As we crept past the sauces a door that none of us had noticed banged open and a zed in a white coat snaked out, reaching for Mina. She put her gun in its face and pulled the trigger twice. I stocked up on chocolate and crisps, head buzzing, throat dry. When I'd finished we headed back towards the tills, seeing five zeds waiting for us by the cigarette counter. Bradley and Kyle put them down without any trouble. This was where we had to take extra care; the counter was next to the front doors that opened out onto the street. Bradley protested as I scrambled over the counter and threw cigarette cartons into the mountainous trolley. Kyle had a close call when a zed popped through the open door and grabbed his arm, but Bradley knocked it down with the butt of his rifle before putting a bullet in its head. Invisible zeds were groaning outside. We were done.

We trotted over to the back doors and out into the glaring sun. Cassie cheered and ran up to me. I kissed her while Kyle shot a couple of zeds that were gliding behind the low car park wall. I kissed Chloe too, a rare treat. Her body was hard and angular against mine, her scent unfamiliar. Kyle and Laura loaded the jeep, the others stood as lookouts. I kept Chloe in my arms, our eyes locked, not speaking.

Zeds were strange for so many reasons. They were an impossibility for one. Everyone knew that the dead couldn't walk, but of course now everyone was a zed. Zeds didn't decompose, their hair and nails didn't grow. They could feel pain, retain memory on a very basic level, and yet they were dead. No blood pressure. No pulse. We'd opened up a few zeds in the past and there the heart was, still as a stone as the zed thrashed around, looking very much alive. Zeds liked to bite but they didn't eat. They weren't as physically strong as we were and they couldn't move too quickly. Zeds weren't very bright. They didn't sleep. They could move with a slow motion liquid grace that hypnotised, but these things weren't the most arresting feature of the zeds. It was their skin, that zed glow.

Some of the zeds didn't have a mark on them. They were the ones who'd caught the virus, or whatever it was. The virus killed most of the animals but only some of the people, though the people quickly came back. These pure zeds fell upon the populace, ripping, biting, creating the messy zeds. Their numbers increased quickly, an exponential zed growth rate. It mushroomed around the world, everything was swallowed up.

The messy zeds were ugly things, skin peeled off them, arms or legs missing, stumbling around with so much intestines hanging out that they would trip over them as they came for you. The pure zeds though, they were something else. The glow made them beautiful. Animated statues of luminous marble moving with that slow grace, like their muscles were made of water, they looked like gods when you first saw them, until they got up close.

Midnight had come and gone. Bradley had disappeared again, Laura and Kyle were in their bedroom. Cassie was sitting on the floor close to the television, watching pornography. We'd found the DVDs, over thirty of them, in the study (now Bradley's library) when we'd moved in. Like Kyle, I'd been impressed at first but the attraction had quickly waned. It was different with Cassie. She'd shown no interest to begin with but over the weeks she'd mutated into an avid fan. She told us that the films helped to improve her technique, which was undeniably true.

Mina lay on the couch, listening to Frank Sinatra, her eyes closed, entranced. She loved Frank and always said that she was glad he'd died long before the zeds came. "It wouldn't do to have him walking around," she'd said, "it just wouldn't be right." We didn't think that the zed virus affected those who were underground. Bradley was adamant about this but none of us wanted to press him on just why he was so sure.

Chloe was sitting next to me, both of us drinking wine. She'd been telling me a little about her life before the zeds, something she'd never discussed with me before.

It was nothing remarkable; she'd been bored and unhappy, unable to relate to people or break down barriers, the usual stuff. Chloe laughed.

"It's so stupid," she said. "I'm as happy here as I was when I was little." She looked at me with her whizzy eyes. "I've found better friends here than the ones I chose in the past."

I'd only fucked Chloe once, and that was when we'd first moved into the house, when we were all scared, lonely, in need of comfort and warmth, so it didn't really count. Chloe put her glass down and I did the same. We started to kiss and when I had the chance I glanced at Cassie to see what she was doing, but she was just staring at the TV with a fixed whizz concentration. I closed my eyes and carried on kissing Chloe while Frank sang about dancing in the dark.

Chloe's blowjob was strangely tender. Cassie liked to perform, using pornographic methods that usually looked better than they felt, while Mina sucked me like a lollipop. Laura was skittish, her touch between a whisper and a caress, smiling all the time. I was still trying to work out which was the best when Chloe stopped and climbed on top of me. Her pubic hair was barely trimmed, another rarity in this house. Her tits pointed to the ceiling and her hands were splayed out, clutching at air.

The bedroom door opened noiselessly. Cassie stood there in a white silk dressing gown. When she saw me looking she raised her eyebrows and dropped the gown to the carpet before turning around. As Chloe frowned in concentration Cassie theatrically licked the middle finger of her right hand and pushed it into her ass. I made a sound and Chloe put her hand on my mouth. She was breathing heavily, sweat glistening on her forehead and between her tits. Cassie was fingering herself and laughing silently, arching her back, sticking her ass out. Chloe moaned, her

21

rhythm jerky, then she fell forward into my arms. She kissed my neck while I watched Cassie over Chloe's shoulder. She took her finger out of her ass and sucked on it innocently, eyes wide and guileless. As Chloe got started again Cassie picked up her dressing gown and let the door close. I turned back to Chloe and kissed her as gently as I could.

We were woken by the suburban sound of a lawnmower. It had to be Bradley. I kissed Chloe's shoulder and stretched, trying a good morning but getting no response. The plan for the day was a vague one, we'd probably ride out of the City again and do some exploring. I crept to the door and moved to the kitchen, making myself toast and coffee, taking them outside into the garden. Bradley was there in a pair of shorts, pushing a lawnmower that was as big as he was. He waved as he went marching by.

After sinking into one of the deckchairs and finishing the toast I took a cigarette from my dressing gown pocket and lit it up. The sunlight was warm, healing me, burning away the whizz cobwebs that were spun throughout my body. I took another sip of coffee, feeling better all the time. Having finished the back lawn Bradley disappeared around the corner to tackle the side. The sound of the mower began to fade. I was running over the night before with Chloe when Cassie and Mina, both naked, appeared from behind me. They lay down like lizards in the sun, chattering about where we would go this afternoon. I stared at them, not listening.

Cassie's body was an exercise in delicate curves, a river of flesh. Her cunt was shaved except for a little bit on the top, carefully shaped and trimmed. Mina had sharper hips and smaller tits. To please Cassie she kept her cunt completely shaved, though she'd complain about razor burn. I shifted in the deckchair, trying to hide my hard-on. Cassie saw me and laughed.

We'd left the main road out of the City twenty minutes ago and were winding through the countryside, faces whipped by overgrown branches, the road smothered in rotting leaves. Chloe was back at the house, concocting in her lab. Bradley was finishing the lawn. We rounded a curve and came to a small bridge that crossed into a tiny village square. There were cottages on either side, a looted corner shop and a pub with broken windows. Six zeds were clustered around a mossy fountain, moving our way. We slowed and came to a stop on the bridge, checking for more. Mina unslung her rifle and took careful aim, then put two of them down.

"Let's go," said Cassie, squeezing me with her legs. She pulled out a pistol as I gunned the engine and headed for the zeds, one of them raising her hands as if in surrender. I whipped the bike into a turn and Cassie began shooting, injuring one and killing another. Kyle had got off his bike and was charging, his sword on high, decapitating the remaining zeds with three strokes. We gathered around the fountain and waited, knowing more would soon be on their way.

"It's a beautiful day," said Laura, gazing at the brilliance of the sky.

"Let's take a photo," suggested Mina, so we took out the Polaroid and set the timer then hurried into a line by our bikes, all smiles, Kyle holding a zed's severed head under his arm. After that I hopped onto the wall around the fountain and lit a cigarette, watching Laura in her silver dress. I hadn't fucked her for nearly a month now.

"Here they come," said Mina, pointing behind me. Seven zeds were approaching, one of them dragging himself across the ground with his hands. The zed bringing up the rear looked pure, an old man with hair like white silk, fixing us with hard eyes, shining like an angel. A zed, a lot like this one had killed a friend of mine, Lewis, bitten his lips off, ripped out his throat while I had watched before running away, screaming.

Cassie and Laura took hold of the swords, rounding the fountain, Cassie bouncing in her trainers, preparing herself. Laura spun her blade in a flashy way and walked slowly up to the first zed, taking up a fighting stance, then the cutting began. Cassie whooped and charged, the girls' hair streaming around them as they sliced, zed blood flying through the air, arms and heads tumbling to the ground, the zeds falling like a house of dead cards. Cassie and Laura met amidst the corpses and clashed their swords together triumphantly, sparks flying from their blades. We all cheered and Mina took another photo.

I'd been on the run from the zeds for three days before I'd first met one of the others. Two of the friends I'd been with had been killed, they'd have been zeds themselves by then. Maybe they were looking for me. I was holed up in a church, crying for some of the time, sleeping for most of it. I hadn't eaten for two days but I'd felt relatively safe; the church was the only place where I hadn't seen any zeds. I might have starved to death if they hadn't finally tumbled in. I'd heard them outside the church door but I'd locked it tight and they couldn't get in. The bastards went round the back instead, crashing through the flimsy back door. Dawn had just been breaking, sunlight beginning to stream in through the windows as I sat weaponless in one of the pews, willing myself to suffer a heart attack or to suddenly go insane, hearing the zeds in the back rooms getting closer. I began crying again and bowed my head. A door opened. There was the unmistakable sound of shuffling feet and a crackled moan that sounded like a laugh. I had my eyes clamped shut and my hands wrapped around a hymn book. My fucking heart wasn't going to burst, I wasn't going to go crazy. I had to act.

When I'd finally looked up I'd seen a zed that used to be a priest, his left shoulder ripped wide open, his arm and neck in tatters. Two more zeds were bringing up the rear. I took some huge breaths and tottered into the aisle, watching the zed get closer. It opened its mouth then closed it like a trap. I snapped and ran for the main door, probably screaming, I can't really remember. The key had turned first time and the door swung open. Another zed was waiting there, a very messy one. One more was coming up the path between the gravestones.

My legs buckled, nerveless. I was yelling hoarsely, wishing I'd been killed before now and didn't have to suffer this. I crawled like a rat back into the church, the zeds closing in on all sides. I'd started retching canary yellow bile, acid raging in my throat, saliva dripping from my mouth in thick strings. The realisation that I was going to get torn up, that I was going to become a zed, hammered through me and I'd puked harder, still crawling to nowhere, only able to croak. I heard a loud thud, then another. Something ran past me. I raised my head and saw a beautiful girl destroying the zed priest's face with an aluminium baseball bat. The zed fell with something leaking from its ears. The girl rushed to the next one and caved its forehead in with a crack. She waited for the last zed, winding the bat up, swinging it violently. The zed fell bonelessly, its nose shattered.

The girl wore black shorts and a tight red T-shirt. Her face was grimy, streaked with tear tracks, her long hair brown and filthy. The baseball bat was covered in dents and clotted with blood, hair and brains. The girl dropped the bat and walked over to me, kneeling down close enough for me to smell the bubblegum on her breath. I opened my mouth to say something then my face crumpled and I started to bawl. The girl held me tight, kissing my hair.

"Hello," I heard her say as I grabbed hold of her waist, never wanting to let go. "My name's Cassie."

Chapter 2

Saturday was always a lazy day, a day when we never went out to look for zeds. We tried to forget about them on weekends. I was sitting under a huge umbrella in the garden, hiding from the sun. Cassie, Mina and Kyle were soaking it up on the loungers. Bradley sat on the swing in a big hat, reading a book about internal combustion engines. Chloe was preparing today's whizz. Laura appeared from the house with a tray of drinks. Gin and tonics for all and a glass of iced water for Bradley. After handing the drinks around Laura took the chair next to mine under the umbrella.

While gulping my drink I listened for the zed wail, but thankfully there was nothing; the sound didn't reach us during the day. Laura lit a cigarette, blowing the smoke up past her fringe. She liked wearing her blonde hair in long pigtails and prized the creamy smoothness of her skin. Laura was the prettiest of the girls, with a little nose and a big smile, too cute to be beautiful. I wasn't as close to her as I'd like to be. Usually the only time we spent face to face was when we were fucking, which only happened when Kyle was around to supervise proceedings. Like Bradley and Chloe, Laura had never been into the basement, although Kyle always did his best to persuade her. She didn't go for girls either, another thing which irked Kyle. He loved to watch Cassie and Mina together (so did I).

"Don't worry about it," Kyle had told me the week before. We'd been lying in bed, watching the sunrise through the window. "All I need is a bit of time. She'll change her mind, I fucking know she will."

"What about?" I'd asked, not really liking the expression on Kyle's face. "The girls or the basement?"

"Both," said Kyle, turning me over and spreading my ass. "Her resistance is crumbling. You just wait and see."

"Aaaaaah!" Bradley jumped off the swing, dropping his book, and ran across the garden into the safety of the house. He may have been ambivalent about the zeds but he was truly terrified of wasps. I laughed along with everyone else and finished my drink. I went into the kitchen to make myself another. Bradley was there, rooting about in the fridge. "My grandfather died from an insect sting," he informed me with his hat hiding his face. "I don't intend tempting fate."

"I think fate's been tempted enough already," I said, spilling some gin as I sloshed it into the glass.

Bradley laughed bitterly. "Yes. Marx would have been proud. Everybody's equal now, the end of false consciousness."

"What?"

"It doesn't matter, forget I spoke. Here's the ice."

Chloe must have been having problems with the whizz because she still hadn't appeared by four o'clock. We were all very drunk by then and the gin was running low. Cassie, Kyle and Mina hadn't put their clothes on yet. Kyle had claimed that he was going to become a naturist for the summer, dressing as God had intended. Cassie had liked the idea, saying that a naked Kyle would keep the zeds away from us. Laura had laughed at that and her drink had gone up her nose. Cassie and Mina had an arm-wrestling competition which Cassie won. I'd cheered her on, Kyle had been supporting Mina. Cassie stood up and flexed her biceps proudly, jutting her hips out. She challenged Laura but Laura shook her head.

"Come on," urged Kyle, none too steady on his feet.

"Let's see who's the strongest."

"I don't think so," Laura said, taking another cigarette from the pack and lighting it.

"Why not?" whined Kyle.

"I'm not much of an arm-wrestler," said Laura flatly.

"Fair enough. What about me, Cass? Fancy your chances?"

"Let's go," she said, lying on the grass. The two locked hands. Cassie started fast, surprising Kyle, but he recovered quickly and it didn't take long for him to push Cassie onto her back. Laughing, he fell on top of her and they began to kiss. Laura crushed her cigarette in the ashtray. Suddenly Kyle jerked away, bellowing. "My dick!" he wailed. "Fucking sunburn!"

"Poor thing," consoled Cassie, "let me see." She moved over Kyle and Laura stood up, walking calmly back into the house. I followed her, swaying, full of gin. I managed to catch up with her in the hallway. "I'm sorry," I said, not knowing why.

Laura turned. "Don't be." She was about to say something else when Chloe came down the stairs from the attic. "Hello lovebirds," she said brightly. She threw Laura a baggie. "Where are the others?" Chloe asked.

"They're fucking in the garden," said Laura.

"Oh. I see. What about Bradley?"

"I'm in here!" came a cry from the living room. Chloe headed for the door. Laura was standing outside her bedroom, biting her lip. I asked if I could come in, not hopefully. Laura looked at the baggie in her hand then motioned me inside. The bedroom was a nightmare in pink, two walls lined with wardrobes, another with a dresser that was covered in make-up appliances and nail polish. I sat on the bed with Laura, not feeling so good; a mixture of lust, guilt and way too much gin. Laura was wearing her short-short white dress with bare feet. She poured some whizz out over a movie magazine and began cutting it into lines with a gold credit card. I caught a glimpse of white underwear that made me lurch as Laura reached back to fetch a note. She handed it to me, Laura looking with eyes so big and blue that they should have been a cliché.

When I snorted two of the lines my nostrils immediately caught fire. I rushed to the kitchen in search of water, grabbing a bottle from the fridge and gulping it down, watching Cassie, Mina and Kyle fucking on the grass. I hurried back to Laura's room to find her gasping, eyes watery. We finished the bottle as the whizz began to hit, slicing through the gin haze, clarifying things. An hour later it was roaring through our veins. Laura was adjusting her hair, her nails electric pink.

"Kyle acts so big," she said, staring manically. "I'm the one who he turns to for comfort, I'm the one who holds him when he's crying in the night. I'm sick of acting like his bloody mother." We were lying against the plush headboard, the ashtray between us. With no one around to distract me I was transfixed onto Laura, her perfume, the shifting of her dress, the ankle bracelet above her right foot, nail polish on her toes. It was difficult equating this girl to the one I'd seen slicing up zeds two days earlier.

"Why do you let Kyle fuck you?" she asked suddenly. "Are you gay?"

"I don't know," I said, taken aback. "I suppose so."

"But you only fucked girls before the zeds?"

"That's right."

"So what's changed?"

"Everything. We don't have limits anymore. We can do whatever we want."

Laura seemed to think about this for a few seconds, looking dubious, before changing the subject. "Do you miss your old friends?"

The whizz gave me a shiver. "Sometimes," I said, trying not to think about seeing Lewis and Mikie getting killed by the zeds, the blood gushing as they were opened up. "What about you?"

"Of course I do," said Laura quickly. She glared at the ceiling and put her arms above her head. Her dress rose another inch. She'd shaved her armpits this morning. "The whizz helps a lot. I can't see how Bradley copes without it. What about love? Do you love Cassie?"

"She's Cassie," I said. "She saved me from the zeds. I love her. One day I'll probably die for her."

Laura sat up and cut some more lines out. We snorted them then Laura told me to follow her, she wanted to see the others. Bradley was still reading in the living room, Chloe was watching a movie. We didn't find anyone in the garden, or in the room I shared with Cassie. Mina's bedroom was next door. That's where they were, the three of them passed out in bed, the sheets pushed onto the floor. The room smelled of sex and gin. Laura sat on the edge of the bed while I leaned against the wall. The whizz rush made balancing tricky. Laura was playing with the baggie in her hand.

"Kyle always pushes me to fuck one of the girls," she said, looking at me. I avoided her eyes, trying to think of something to say. "Shame he's sleeping," smiled Laura, opening the baggie. She moved to Cassie, who was lying on her back and breathing heavily. Carefully Laura poured whizz over Cassie's tits, sprinkling it liberally over her nipples. Laura pushed her hair back and leaned over, her dress riding up, her tiny pink tongue flicking out. She licked Cassie's tits slowly, cleaning up the whizz, leaving a glistening trail of spit. She sucked long on Cassie's nipples, hardening them into fat points. Cassie didn't move, dead to the world. When she'd finished Laura stood up unsteadily and walked to the door. "Come with me," she said.

In the street the zeds were dropping like flies. I shot another three before I had to reload the rifle. Bradley, Chloe and Kyle were inside the pharmacy. Their list included pads, tampons, Polaroid films, vitamins, soap, contraceptive pills, downers, uppers, painkillers, shaving foam, razors, KY Jelly and sunblock. Mina was standing by the jeep with the Uzi, Laura and Cassie had the SA80s. After we'd cleared the visible zeds Cassie began looking curiously at the shop next to the pharmacy. It sold electrical goods and was protected by steel shutters that were spattered with zed gore. Cassie did something to her gun and started firing at the shop, stopping when the shutters were in tatters. "What's she doing?" asked a puzzled Mina. Cassie jumped inside and Laura shot a zed that glided out of a side street. It wasn't long before Cassie came back. In one hand she was waving a flashy looking camcorder.

When the others came out of the pharmacy Bradley wanted to know what had happened. Cassie explained while Kyle and Mina loaded the jeep. The rest of us watched for zeds. I spotted one and put it down, turning to see Bradley following Cassie back into the electrical shop. I was just beginning to grow worried when they came back out, carrying a box each. "An editing suite," Bradley said, looking pleased. "Cassandra's a genius." Cassie kissed Bradley's cheek and climbed into the back of the jeep. Laura and I took down a couple of not bad looking zeds that had wandered on the scene.

On the way home Laura asked Cassie what she was going to do with all the new gear. "What do you think?" said Kyle, laughing. "She's going to make movies! Isn't that right?"

"It's true," said Cassie. "We're going to have some

more fun."

"What kind of films are you going to make?" asked Chloe suspiciously.

"Cassie'll make the kind of movies she likes best," answered Kyle. He wrapped an arm around Laura's shoulders. "She's going to make us famous! We're going to be stars! What's your acting like, Laura?"

"Poor," she said, looking out of the window at the empty street that was passing by.

"How about a title?" Mina asked Cassie.

"Let me guess," said Kyle. "Cassie's Awakening? Mina Meets Her Master? Teenage Bisexual Nymphomaniac Speedfreaks?"

Cassie sighed. "Tell it to the zeds, Kyle."

Bradley spent the night in the library, working out how to use the new equipment. The rest of us were whizzing in the living room. Laura, Mina and Kyle were dancing to the music that was booming from the waist-high speakers. Chloe seemed happy by herself in the corner. I was sitting with Cassie. She'd been impressed by the bite and scratch marks that Laura had put on my skin during Saturday night. When I'd told Cassie what Laura had done to her while she'd been sleeping she'd been even more impressed, though I made her promise not to tell Kyle.

"Stop staring at her," I said.

"Oh shut up, Alex. You're the one who's been making goo-goo eyes at her for the past two days."

"I have?"

"Of course you have."

"Really?"

"Fucking hell. Yes, really. You're such a puppy sometimes." Cassie continued to watch Laura closely, who was dancing with Mina now, hair flying. "Women aren't

33

made from candy-floss, you know," Cassie told me. "There's something inside Laura that's starting to come out."

"What kind of thing?"

"A sex thing," said Cassie promptly.

"Are you sure?"

"Course I am. Trust me on this, I'm a girl with powerful instincts. All Laura needs is a little time, a lot of whizz and a friendly hand to guide her." Cassie lit up a cigarette, smiling. "I've been waiting for this to happen," she said. "It's been coming for a while. Things are going to hot up, Alex, just wait and see." Laura saw Cassie looking and waved. Cassie laughed and waved back.

At dawn we swallowed our downers and dragged Bradley grumbling out of bed. He came with us up to the balcony and the seven of us watched the sun come up, burning away the milky clouds. I took Laura's hand and pretended not to notice Cassie rolling her eyes at Mina.

"Where are we going?" asked Chloe.

"I don't know," answered Kyle, hands on the balcony railings.

"We're not going anywhere," said Bradley defiantly.

"What about when we're older?" Mina asked us all.

"What about it?" Bradley demanded.

"My parents told me that when I grew up I'd become someone different."

"I think living through the Apocalypse matures a person," said Bradley. "I know that I don't feel thirteen anymore, more like thirty-three. What about you, Cassandra?"

"I feel like I'm six," Cassie said. She was fourteen, the same age as Laura. I was a year older, as was Kyle. Mina was sixteen, Chloe had just turned seventeen. It wasn't young or old, it was just life. As Bradley had said, the end of the world made you grow up fast. I squeezed Laura's hand and she squeezed back hard.

Shopping anywhere near the City Centre was always risky. It was the focus point of zed activity, where the wail we could hear at night originated from. Cassie had told us about her plan early this morning. She wanted to get some costumes for the movies she was going to make and the only place she could think of that sold them was a place called Trash, which stood on the centre's fringes, just outside the pedestrianised highstreets.

"You're out of your mind," Kyle had said. "That's where all the fucking zeds are, thousands and thousands of them. They'd rip us to pieces."

"Trash is on a road," pointed out Cassie. "We'd be in and out, two minutes, tops. I talked to Bradley about it."

"I bet he laughed his ass off," said Kyle.

"He said that as long as we all went then there wouldn't be a problem." Cassie stood and leaned across the kitchen table, both of us staring down her top. "I need you both to come," she'd said.

The seven of us set off before noon, packed inside the sweltering jeep. I was surprised that Laura and Chloe had agreed to this but there they were in the front, chatting about traffic congestion. I was squashed between Bradley and Mina. Cassie was next to the window, Kyle on her left, stroking her thigh. This was the closest to the centre we'd been since the zeds came and I was crackling with nerves and whizz. Chloe took us out of the Gardens and onto the roads into town.

The journey was a tortuous one. The roads to the centre were choked with empty cars, most of them with their doors hanging open. The zeds were out in force, wandering under the sun. Surprisingly, most of them didn't pay much attention to us. I lost count of the number of times that the road was impassable and Chloe had to back up to find another route. It was stifling in the jeep, the open windows not seeming to make much difference either way. Bradley complained about the heat the most, followed by me.

"Not again," groaned Chloe. This time the road was blocked by an overturned truck and two crashed cars. As we slowed down the zeds began moving in. Bradley, Laura and Cassie shot them with their pistols while Chloe turned us around. A zed's hands thumped on the back of the jeep before we drove away. I was beginning to doubt whether we'd ever get there, we were stupid agreeing to it, though I rarely said no to Cassie; she could be very persuasive. Bradley was immune to her charms though, and he'd said that this fucking journey wouldn't be a problem. Obviously this debacle was down to him.

"This is your fault, Bradley," I told him.

He turned to face me, sharp face sweating in the heat, but he didn't say anything. No one did, we just carried on through side street after side street, zed numbers increasing constantly, more and more of them standing in the road, clawing at the jeep as we drove by. I was getting car-sick, or maybe it was heat stroke, I didn't know. Chloe yelled in frustration as we came to yet another blocked road. Back we went, shooting zeds all the way.

"Take this right," said Bradley.

"We just went down there," snapped Chloe.

"The heat has fried your wits," Bradley said sharply. "Take this right."

Chloe took it, weaving through the cars and zeds.

"Now this left, and the next right."

We came out onto one of the roundabouts that led to the centre. We all cheered, except Bradley, who just looked out of the window, his face blank. Chloe drove us past the shattered traffic lights, crossing lanes to avoid the pile-ups, then through another roundabout. There were huge numbers of zeds about now, I'd never seen this many before and I couldn't help feeling that stopping the jeep any time soon would be a bad idea.

"We're nearly there," said Cassie. "Get ready. Chloe; that shop with the red sign."

"I see it." Chloe spun the wheel and pulled us up. We threw open the doors and started shooting into the zed tide. Cassie and Mina blew the shop windows out and went inside. The zeds were falling fast but their numbers kept increasing. The two girls came back, their arms loaded with slim boxes. They threw them in the jeep then ran back inside. I stood on the road with the rifle, the pile of corpses in front of me growing all the time. The zeds were getting close. Mina leapt out of the shop with some clothes wrapped in plastic over one arm. Cassie followed, looking pleased. She threw the clothes into the jeep and shot two zeds with her pistol. The two girls ducked into the jeep and we all stopped shooting.

"Time to go!" hollered Mina. I stood there for a second, the terrible sound of thousands of wailing zeds suddenly audible after the gunfire. Just how many were there before us? A thousand? They were still moving in, slow but eager, glowing with that zed light, all eyes marking us. "What the fuck are you doing?" Kyle screamed in my face. "Let's go!" I jumped in sudden terror and raced to the jeep, zeds too close behind. I dived in after Kyle and slammed the door behind me as Chloe ploughed a way through the throng, the zeds not backing off, surrounding the jeep, cracking under the wheels. Their faces blazed in at us, teeth bared, shining zed hands with nails like glass scratching at the windows.

Cassie stayed tight-lipped about the things she'd brought home. "You'll see soon enough," was all we could get out of her before she disappeared into her room with Mina. Kyle, Bradley and Chloe played cards in the living room while I sat in the garden with Laura, drinking whisky and smoking cigarettes. It was past seven o'clock, the sky still bright, the trees rustling. I thought the whisky tasted horrible but the effect made up for it. Laura poured another glass and took a gulp, her face glowing. She looked at me. "Did you tell Cassie what I did on Saturday night?"

"Yes," I said, "I'm sorry. She won't tell Kyle."

Laura shrugged and rolled her glass between her hands. "I don't care anymore. Everything's breaking up." She picked something up from the grass and looked at it. It was the Polaroid that Mina had taken the week before, Laura and Cassie brandishing the swords, sparks in the air, dead zeds over the ground. In the picture Laura was grinning savagely, a different person. Cassie looked just the same. We drank some more whisky, waiting for something. I could have done with some whizz but we'd all agreed that we would take two days off each week, eating plenty of food, trying to fatten up. I didn't know whether it helped or not. Then Laura was kissing me, her tongue over mine, hand on my stomach.

"Beautiful," I heard Bradley say from behind us. "A wonderful screen couple, you put Bogart and Bacall to shame. Such chemistry! Keep at it! The camera loves, it adores you both."

Laura looked up, puzzled, then her eyes widened. "Bradley! No!" Laura recoiled then fell flat on the grass, her dress way up.

"Fantastic!" proclaimed Bradley, coming into view with a camcorder attached to his face. "Pratfall! I didn't know that you did slapstick as well as love scenes, Laura."

"I don't," she said. "Stop pointing that thing at me."

"I have to have something on film so I can learn how to edit."

"Piss off."

"As charming as she is beautiful. What about a song? A soft shoe shuffle? How about stand-up? You know; 'A funny thing happened to me on the way to the morgue yesterday'. Punchline?"

Laura was standing up now, hands on her hips. "Bradley, if you don't take that camera away I'll kick you over the fence and feed you to the zeds." She looked like she meant it. Bradley must have thought so too because he then turned the camera on me. Up until now I'd been finding all this pretty funny but I was beginning to change my mind.

"And so," Bradley began, "we have Alexander the Great; zed-killer, stud and intellectual. Tell me, do you model yourself on your more famous but less illustrious predecessor?"

"What?" Bradley always confused me.

"Well, perhaps you've never heard of him," said Bradley. Laura wasn't looking so angry anymore. In fact, she was beginning to laugh. "He's blushing!" howled Bradley. "So endearing. I think I'm beginning to understand his effect on women. Have you ever longed to be on the silver screen?"

"Not really," I said, pinned in the deckchair.

"Such a shame. You're a natural, I can tell. I do know, however, that you enjoy psychoanalysis. Would you do us the honour of expounding your deconstruction on the pleasure principle, and quite possibly beyond?"

"The what?" I'd rather have faced a zed, armed only with a toothpick, than carry on with this, but what could I do?

"The pleasure principle," repeated Bradley patiently. "I've heard you wax lyrical on the subject many times. Can you explain the basic tenets to us? You look confused, Alex. That's right, have a drink. Could it be that your usual eloquence is only provided by the prodigious amounts of amphetamines that you ceaselessly imbibe? Could it be that the personalities belonging to the people in this house revolve solely around this stimulant, magnifying the darker elements of the libido and increasing the innate violent impulses in us all? Surely not, it could never be that simple. Come, Alex, prove us wrong."

Cassie saved me again. She came bouncing out of the house in tiny denim shorts and a stripy T-shirt, smiling broadly. "How's the filming going, Bradley? Have you got enough yet?"

Bradley turned the camera on Cassie. "Tragically, no. Another few minutes should do the trick. Your man here's been a great help." Cassie laughed and kissed me loudly on the cheek, then she turned my face to hers and kissed me properly. "Two in as many minutes!" Bradley cried. "How does he do it?"

We hit the whizz hard on the weekend. I spent an hour in the basement with Cassie and Kyle, Mina staying upstairs with Frank Sinatra. Not long after we came back upstairs Chloe began whispering with Kyle in the chair by the corner. By midnight they'd disappeared to her room. Cassie talked closely with Laura on the couch, hand on her leg, as I watched Mina painting her nails with whizz precision. Her dyed black hair was back in a ponytail and she wore an expensive looking blue dress. Mina loved Cassie as much as I did. We'd found her the day after Cassie had saved me in the church.

When the zeds appeared Mina had stayed locked in her house, using her father's pistol to drop the zeds that came too close. She'd been alone for over a week and only had two bullets left. We couldn't miss the pile of bodies in front of the house and we'd stopped our bikes to take a

40

look. Three messy zeds appeared from nowhere and began shuffling towards us. I'd taken the baseball bat and put them down while Cassie called to the open window upstairs. Less than ten seconds later the front door was thrown open and Mina had jumped weeping into Cassie's arms.

"What's so funny?" Mina asked me, looking up from her nails.

"Just remembering how we met," I said.

"Hmm. I don't remember laughing much at the time. I don't remember you laughing either. You had that baseball bat with brains all over it."

"It was Cassie's."

"Whatever." Mina went back to her nails, troubled. "I'm glad you both got there when you did," she said. "I wasn't far from ending it all."

"I'm glad you didn't," I said lamely.

"Me too. What do you think?"

"Very nice. Purple's your colour."

At three o'clock Cassie and Mina were dancing around the room, bouncing off the walls. I was sitting with Laura again. We shared some lines and talked about Bradley and his camera, laughing. Then Laura told me that she'd asked Cassie why she enjoyed going down into the basement. Cassie had said that Laura was taking things too seriously, that the basement was no big deal, it was just fun like everything else.

"I still can't help thinking it's sick," Laura said without conviction.

I lit a cigarette, thinking. "Basement fun *is* sick fun," I said, "but so is the fun we have outside. This is a sick city now, a sick world. You have to become a little sick yourself to survive in it."

We saw Cassie and Mina run into each other and kiss. Cassie put a hand up Mina's dress and the two of them fell to the carpet, screeching. Laura sat back and put a boot up onto the coffee table. "Sickness is infectious," she said.

Chapter 3

Tuesday afternoon found us breaking into the biggest house we could find on our street. I was with Cassie and Laura. Chloe and Kyle were in bed yet again. Mina was editing with Bradley. The three of us had taken as much whizz as we could, grabbed a couple of pistols each and a few tools, then we'd gone exploring. It was always different to kill some zeds in the confinement of a house, it added to the buzz. On the street it was easy, there was so much space, but in a hallway or on a landing a zed could be a metre away and you wouldn't know it, not until you looked behind a door.

The street was empty, dead. The loudest sound was made by our feet thwapping on the road. After twenty minutes of walking we found the place we wanted. The house stood three storeys tall, the garden wild, surrounded by a wilting fence. The front gate was unlocked. We were all excited, whizzing to the limit, senses tuned and hot in the sun. We went in single file along the jungly path that led away from the drive and around the side of the house. Our first zed of the day was wandering in the garden, his shirt ripped open, his chest ripped open. Cassie put him down, the gunshot echoing in the stillness around us.

The back door stood open. We crept inside, Cassie leading the way. The kitchen was empty, the floor muddy with zed footprints. "Anybody home?" called Laura, making Cassie laugh. Something thumped upstairs in answer. We searched the downstairs rooms, finding nothing but clutter and long-dried pools of blood. Next we went up the stairs to the first floor, guns ready. The landing was a mess, scattered clothes everywhere and a huge amount of old blood spread across the carpet. This was probably where the zed in the garden had been torn up. Laura opened the first door, a bedroom. Empty. Same with the next one. The other doors were open already, smudged with rusty handprints.

We found nothing in the huge bathroom. By now I was exchanging nervous glances with Laura. The zeds were here, we knew it. They were hiding, waiting for the right moment when we'd be off our guard, waiting to rip out our throats and peel our skulls. "Stay cool, both of you," ordered Cassie as we walked back into the hallway, then a zed was sliding in low, its mouth torn into a grin, and Cassie shot it through the eye. The zed fell and was still. We stepped over the body into the next room, tension released by the killing. A zed that had once been a maid was coming for us, her throat and face mangled. "Nice uniform," said Cassie as I shot it with Laura. "Very sexy." Now there was only one more floor to go.

I jumped when I reached the stairs. A female zed stood at the top, silhouetted against the window. Laura was about to shoot it when Cassie put a hand on her arm. "Wait. Let her come down." We backed off as the zed croaked something and started down the stairs.

"What are we waiting for?" Laura asked me, but I was staring at the zed, who had stopped halfway down and was regarding us with burning eyes. Her hair was long and blonde and clotted with blood. More was smeared across her mouth and her nightdress had been soaked in it. When she was alive she'd probably been very pretty, but now, with the glow inside her skin and her zed eyes, she was beautiful.

"Let's see if she's pure," said Cassie. "I'll get behind her and knock her down, you two grab her arms, keep her on the floor."

The zed's eyes narrowed as she continued down the stairs, moving without sound, one hand trailing along the banister, the other flexing itself, bloody fingers rippling. Cassie disappeared into a bedroom while I followed Laura back down the hallway. The zed reached the bottom and looked at where Cassie had gone, debating whether to follow.

"Hey!" said Laura, clapping her hands. The zed turned and glided at us, the movement so liquid it looked like she wasn't moving at all. Cassie leapt from the doorway onto the back of the zed. She thumped to the carpet, mewling. I held her down with Laura, the zed's struggles surprisingly powerful. Kneeling on her back, Cassie took her handcuffs from her pocket and we forced the zed's arms into place behind her back, moving to avoid the snapping mouth.

Cassie clicked the handcuffs tight around the zed's wrists. "Now hold her head," said Cassie, breathing heavily. She reached behind and pulled out a black rubber gag with a tongue depressor attached. We grabbed the head and pulled it up, the zed snarling and manic. Cassie pulled the gag over the zed's mouth and fitted the straps at the back, muffling the zed's wails.

"What happens now?" asked Laura, eyes wide.

"Now we check the merchandise," answered Cassie. We flipped the zed onto her back and Cassie ripped open the nightdress. The zed was still struggling but the handcuffs made her powerless. She tossed her head as Cassie finished ripping and the zed was revealed. Her body was unmarked, pure, the skin's glow unfeasibly erotic. Cassie ran her hands up the zed's body and over her tits.

"Implants," noted Cassie dreamily. She turned to me and, knowing the drill, I helped force the zed's legs apart as Cassie moved down, pushing her face into the zed's cunt, keeping it there as the zed arched her back into a bow, banging her head on the carpet.

Cassie drew away and I took off my clothes, hard-on aching, whizz racing through my blood. I prised the zed's legs open again and began fucking her hard, pressing her shoulders to the floor, keeping her down. The zed's cunt was like ice, the cold seeping through my cock, tightening my balls, freezing my stomach, my heart, my brain. The zed's eyes were rolling wildly, her mouth straining at the gag, legs high and kicking.

Laura was still kneeling by the zed's head. She'd tried to move away but Cassie had stepped behind her and put restraining hands on her shoulders. Cassie trailed her fingers over Laura's arms and stroked her hair gently. She began whispering into Laura's ear, pausing to plant kisses on her neck. I fucked the zed as hard as I could, grabbing her cold arms and shaking her, smelling the blood in her hair, turning to watch Cassie smile and whisper, seeing her pull up Laura's pink dress. Laura was staring glassy-eyed, face scarlet, breathing in shallow gasps.

The zed's convulsions were getting stronger and I was having trouble keeping her down. She twisted like a snake, kicking higher and whipping her head back and forth. Cassie ran her hand up Laura's leg, over her hip. My orgasm began to build and Laura cried out softly as Cassie's hand slipped into her underwear. Cassie's fingers began working inside the white cotton. Laura was panting, head held high, eyes locked onto the struggling zed. I grabbed fistfuls of the zed's hair, forcing her head still. She glared up at Laura and the two locked eyes, the zed's gaze fierce, unblinking. Laura opened her mouth as if to say something and I spilled an icy orgasm into the zed, untangling myself from her legs and collapsing on the floor, shivering.

Cassie took her hand from Laura's underwear and wiped her glistening fingers over the zed's stomach. Laura got up and turned away, head in her hands. I dressed slowly, still cold from the zed, panting. The three of us pulled the zed up and walked her down the stairs. The zed was taller than all of us. Cassie pushed her through the house and out into the garden. We walked home, the zed unable to help following us, driven by her hunger. Laura lit a cigarette and dragged deep as Cassie began skipping down the street, singing a nonsense song about how much fun the zeds could be.

When we went to bed that night we took Laura with us, pumped full of downers and gin. I fucked her slowly while Cassie watched, Laura lying passive, her eyes closed, arms thrown back over her head. When the pills began kicking in I started losing my hard-on so I rolled away. Cassie took over, face in Laura's blonde cunt, pushing her legs back. Laura opened her drugged eyes and gazed at me distantly. "I'm floating," she whispered. "It's pretty, so pretty, the clouds." Laura closed her eyes and smiled wide at the ceiling, drifting away.

Bradley's all-time favourite film was Casablanca. We all watched it on Wednesday night, lost in a haze of pills. Chloe and Kyle were cuddling by the fireplace. They seemed to have fallen in love, something I was finding difficult to believe. There they were though, eyeball to misty eyeball, grinning at each other, lost. We'd given Laura more pills than the rest of us and she was lying on the couch with her head on Cassie's lap, apparently passed out. Cassie was stroking Laura's face with one hand and smoking a cigarette with the other. I'd been worried that the change in Laura was going to cause problems but Kyle hadn't noticed and Mina didn't seem to care. I was sitting on the floor with her, sharing a box of stale popcorn. Bradley was lying on his stomach not far from the television, chin resting on his hands. He cried through the final scene. He always cried through the final scene, he claimed it was excellent therapy.

"Therapy is important," he'd told me, "it's, well, therapeutic. You use a lot of it yourself, don't you?"

"Why do you ask so many questions?"

"Because I'm interested in things. I like to learn. Education is extremely important, even now. Especially now."

"Is education as important as therapy?"

"Good question. Education used to be far more important, but priorities have changed. Both mean far more than they ever did, but I think that therapy is in the ascendancy. The point can't be stressed enough."

After the movie Bradley blew his nose and put some of his terrible pop music on the stereo. I was getting sick of the bad popcorn. "This is disgusting," Mina said, continuing to eat it. I lit a cigarette to stop myself. Laura woke up, dazed. She tried to sit up but Cassie gently pushed her head down and Laura didn't have the strength to force things so she gave up, closing her eyes again.

"I'm going to start filming soon," announced Cassie.

"Who's going to be in it?" mumbled Laura.

"Mina, Kyle and Alex." Cassie cast a glance at the scene by the fireplace. "That is, if I can prise Kyle away from Chloe. I won't be too ambitious, it's only going to be a short. Ten minutes, set in the garden on a beautiful summer's day. Bradley, are you sure you won't be the camera man?"

"You can be the camera man," said Bradley. "I'll edit the thing, but I certainly won't be present at the filming. I wouldn't be able to hold the camera still through laughing."

I was on my way to bed when Kyle cornered me in the hallway. He didn't look happy. "I've moved my things into Chloe's room," he said quietly. "We've found something special together. Don't laugh, it's true, you've seen the way we are. It's beautiful. Only thing is, I haven't told Laura yet. I don't want to upset her, you know? I'll tell her myself but could you, like, prepare the ground? Soften the blow? No one likes being alone, I don't want her to feel rejected. Hey, what's so fucking funny?"

I wanted to say something but Kyle would probably get ugly so I just pushed open the bedroom door. Kyle frowned, then looked inside. Cassie was sitting up in bed with another cigarette, apparently alone. When she saw Kyle she smiled and pulled back the blanket. Kyle's jaw dropped when he saw Laura wrapped around Cassie, asleep. He flushed and turned to me, then he laughed, probably because of all the downers in his system. "You fucking bastards," he said, still laughing, then he walked to Chloe's room, shaking his head.

The reason I was out slicing zeds early on Thursday morning was down to Cassie. She'd called me into the kitchen along with Mina and Kyle. "You're all going to be working together," she'd said, deadpan. "I want you to bond." We'd all laughed at that but Cassie's face hadn't changed. She sent us out with the swords and a pistol each, telling us to, "Help each other out. Rely on each other."

"We do that anyway," Kyle had complained.

Cassie wouldn't be moved. "This is just the three of you, it's different. Off you go. Don't come back until you've killed some zeds."

The three of us stood in a triangle, over ten zeds moving in, all of them messy, some messier. We cut them down without any trouble. The road began to flow with zed blood and we stepped away. Mina wondered aloud whether we'd bonded yet.

"Could be," I said. "Say, what's your score?"

"Don't know," shrugged Mina. "What's yours?"

"No idea."

"We've all passed a hundred," said Mina. "That was the point of the whole thing."

We walked down the street on the way back to the house. Kyle pointed out a zed that had got itself stuck inside a car. It was fumbling with the door, trying to get out. Kyle shot it with his pistol. "Shit," said Mina, tapping me on the shoulder. I turned to see a large group of zeds behind us, maybe twenty. Kyle whistled through his teeth. It was eerie to see how easily zeds could creep up on you, finding strength in their numbers. Now another six were coming from the direction of the house. A few of the zeds began moaning but most stayed silent, moving implacably forward. I shot the six zeds in front, Kyle and Mina took down the larger group behind. More appeared from the side, three or four, obscured by the parked cars. Kyle ran out of bullets. So did Mina. There were at least eight zeds left standing and more were only injured, climbing to their feet or crawling towards us. I killed another four then my gun clicked empty.

"I think we should leave," Kyle said, sword ready. "I feel bonded enough."

The zeds continued to grope forward, surrounding us, more of them appearing all the time. This was getting serious. We looked at each other to centre ourselves then charged where the zed circle was thinnest, chopping our way out, zed arms and hands falling to the road, still clutching. We fled down the street, suddenly delirious, waving out swords, leaving the zeds behind. One of them surprised us by jumping out from behind the trees but Mina moved in and sliced its head off. She kicked the head to Kyle, who passed it to me. I dribbled the head down the street, leaving tracks of blood and brain. I passed the head to Mina, who knocked it back to Kyle. He swung his foot back and booted the head through the open window of a car that had crashed into a garden wall. "Goal!" screamed Kyle, whipping off his T-shirt and waving it above his head. We all laughed and ran home, celebrating victory.

I was standing naked in the garden with Kyle, feeling like a fool. Laura was still doped up, lolling on the swing. I'd asked Cassie when she was going to stop popping the pills down Laura's throat but Cassie had just pinched my cheek and told me not to interfere, Laura was going to be just fine, she needed this time to adjust. Right now Cassie was arguing with Mina about shoes. "I'm not putting those things on," Mina was saying for the tenth time. "I don't mind doing this, it might be fun, but not when I'm wearing those. Look at them, they're hideous."

"You don't understand," said Cassie patiently. She picked the shoes up, keeping her eyes on Mina. "This isn't a fashion thing, we're dealing with pornography here. The rules are all different. Stilettos are essential."

"I don't care," Mina said, crossing her arms.

"Please, Mina. Do this for me."

"No."

"I can't do it without you."

"And I can't do it with those things on."

"Yes you can."

"Forget it."

Cassie sat down on the grass next to Mina and began speaking to her quietly. I tried my best to listen in but I couldn't catch the words. Kyle was looking quizzically at me. I shrugged and turned away. Five minutes later Mina undressed and strapped the shoes onto her feet, her face like thunder. Cassie clapped her hands briskly, making Laura raise her head, then Cassie took her place behind the camera.

"Mina, just lie there in the sun, catch up on your tan.

Boys, it's time to get it up. Come on, you know you can do it. Look at Mina, isn't she sexy? See those shoes?

"Mina, give the boys some encouragement. That's the idea. See, it's working already. All right, that's good. Now we're ready. Alex, get out of shot, you're not on yet. You too, Kyle. OK. Mina, are you ready? Feeling good? That's excellent. You look great Mina, you're going to be fine. Are we ready? All right then. No tricks, let's go."

It all went so well until the final scene, what Cassie called the money shot. "You boys just stand there," she said. We'd been at it for well over an hour and we were all exhausted. "Just stand there and do what you do best. When it's time remember to aim at Mina's mouth."

"Do we really have to do this part?" asked Mina.

"Of course we do," said Cassie. "This is the most important bit."

"I can't come standing up," said Kyle.

Cassie threw up her hands. "Yes you can! I've seen you do it. Now get going."

It took me nearly five minutes to come, and when I did it wasn't as much as I, or Cassie, had hoped. When Mina had finished with me, only grimacing a little, I staggered out of shot and collapsed onto the grass, my dick raw, my arm numb. I couldn't believe that some people had actually used to do this for a living.

"My eye, my eye!" Mina suddenly shrieked. "It's burning! Fuck, I'm fucking blind!" Cassie dropped the camera and ran to fetch some water. I looked and saw Kyle standing there dumbfounded, come still oozing from his dick while Mina howled, rolling on the grass with her hands covering her face.

"I'm sorry," said Kyle. "I didn't mean to, it just came out wrong." Cassie rushed past him with a bottle of water. She knelt before Mina and forced her hands away from her face. Cassie washed out Mina's eye and cleaned her face up with a towel. Mina started to cry and Cassie held her, rocking her to and fro, looking disappointed.

That evening Bradley began editing Cassie's movie, saying that it should take him a day or so. Mina recovered quickly and after a few lines she was laughing about the whole thing. I wanted to go out on the bikes again tomorrow, feel the wind in my face, do some exploring. Cassie, Mina and Laura all agreed to come. We didn't know about Kyle. He was dancing smoochily with Chloe, his hands on her ass. Laura was sunk back on the couch, leaning on Cassie. She gave Laura another pill and kissed her hair. Laura drank some wine and began telling us in a faraway voice about how she'd seen her first zed.

"I'd been coming home from school," she said, closing her eyes. "There was a commotion in the street, people running, running everywhere. My mum came rushing out of our house, waving at me. That's when I began to get scared. Then I saw Mr Eliot, who lived next door. He'd been ill for a couple of days, lots of people had, and now he was all white, glowing. His hands and face had blood all over them. My mum tripped and he fell on top of her, I didn't know what he was doing. Mum started to scream. I ran to help her and pushed Mr Eliot off. There was so much blood, I slipped in it and fell. Mum's face was bitten, all bloody. I started screaming for help but by now the street was nearly empty.

"When I tried to pull my mum into our house Mr Eliot grabbed her and bit her leg. I saw Donna, she was only eight, and she was glowing as well, moving in this weird way, like her bones were melting. I heard sirens and Donna grabbed my arm. Her hand was freezing. I pushed her away before she could bite me, I think mum was dead by then. Mr Eliot started coming for me so I ran into the house and slammed the door. There were more sirens all the time but the police never came."

Cassie hugged Laura and kissed her mouth, pulling her down again onto her lap. "They're still out there," Laura said, her voice growing fainter, "all of them, walking around. Waiting for us." Her face became slack and Cassie lit a cigarette, smiling at me. We carried Laura to bed then went back to the living room for more lines.

"Laura's being born again," Cassie told me. "Tomorrow she gets back on the whizz."

The grass rose waist high around us, rolling away as far as we could see. We'd left the bikes on the side of the road and were racing for a line of trees ahead. Mina had said they shielded a stream she used to go to when she was younger. She was the fastest of us, ponytail flying. I wasn't far behind though I was losing ground all the time. Cassie and Laura were running together behind me. I tried to put on a final burst of speed but I was flat out and burning in the heat, muscles losing it.

Mina disappeared into the trees. I burst through them a few seconds later, crashing into her. We laughed and kissed, exhausted, tasting each other's sweat. The stream here had grown into a wide pool, the still water looking deep. The overhanging trees protected us from the sun's glare. We stripped and dived in, the water welcoming ice, stopping our breath and squeezing our hearts. I came spluttering to the surface. Cassie and Laura were standing naked on the bank, Laura dipping her toe into the water.

"No way," she said, "too cold." Cassie pushed her and Laura fell in with a shriek. Cassie dived in with precision.

We swam and splashed and looked for fish. We spouted water like whales and collected stones from the bottom. The girls tried to drown me and very nearly succeeded. I had to climb out of the pool then, my strength gone. I scrambled up the bank and through the trees so I could dry in the sun. Our bikes were twinkling in the distance. Nothing moved, in the sky or on the ground. The only sounds came from the pool, Laura calling for help and Cassie laughing, water splashing, and these sounds soon died away into nothing. When I was dry I walked back through the trees and saw the girls lying face down in the water, their hair fanning out and intermingling, blonde, red and black. I called out to them but they didn't move. They just floated limply in the water, pretending they were dead.

The walk back to the bikes seemed to take hours. We talked about what name we should choose for the zed we'd found in the big house. Eventually we decided on Laura's choice, which was Kaylan. Cassie was hoping that Bradley would have finished his editing job by the time we got home. She wanted to premiere her movie that night. "Maybe you'll be in my next one," Cassie said hopefully to Laura.

"Maybe," Laura answered, watching the sky. Cassie put an encouraging arm around her shoulders and we walked on in silence until we reached the bikes. On the journey home we saw plenty of zeds but we ignored them, wanting to get back to the house as quickly as we could. When we arrived Chloe the chemist was waiting for us, hands overflowing with whizz, welcoming us home.

Many generous lines later and the mood was good. I raced around the house a few times with Kyle in a fun but futile attempt to work off some of the boundless energy that the whizz had given me. We sank gin and tonics and I danced with our chemist until I fell over Laura and hit my head on the floor, hard, though I hardly felt it. Mina told us a funny story about how she'd lost her virginity in the men's toilets at a snooker hall in the City with a boy named Brian, who'd cried after he'd fucked her, thanking her for the most beautiful moment of his life, sitting on the toilet with his jeans around his ankles.

We all jabbered at each other for another two hours, exchanging more stories, swapping theories about how the zeds began, where they came from. Mina advocated alien space rays, Kyle hinted darkly at some kind of religious punishment, the rest of us thought it had to be a genetically modified biological weapon that some genius had dropped or fired into the sky. What was it like to be a zed? How long could they last? How long could *we* last? Would the insects take over the world? Which ones? Bees? Ants? Spiders?

After it grew dark Bradley appeared with a tape in his hand. Cassie leapt up and kissed him on the forehead. He put the tape in the machine and left, face unreadable. We all did more lines then Cassie put the tape on with gusto. I was sure that Bradley would have played a few tricks but I'd been completely wrong. No spliced footage or unsuitable soundtrack, no overdubbing with animal noises, not even a sarcastic nature documentary voice-over. In a way it was disappointing, and frustrating that I found Bradley so unpredictable. The film was just ten or so minutes of Mina in stilettos, getting fucked in a variety of ways and places by two faceless people. To be honest, it was kind of dull.

Cassie obviously thought differently. She cut huge amounts of whizz for everyone then took Mina's hand and pulled her out of the room. Fifteen minutes later the rest of us were choked by the whizz, gasping for air. Mina came back in with the camcorder in her hand, telling us that she was going down into the basement. Kyle stood up first. It took me a few seconds longer, my senses whizz-scrambled like never before. I held my hand out to Laura. She took it of course, her face an empty shell.

We moved into the kitchen like scarecrows, leaving Chloe smoking a cigarette. Laura's hand was cool and dry in mine. Mina opened the basement door, clicked on the light and went inside. We all followed. The first thing you saw when you went into the basement was the thick red carpet at the bottom of the steps. The first thing you heard was the rattling of chains. The room was huge and we'd painted the walls black to drink in the light.

As soon as we reached the bottom the zeds tried to come for us. There was Marian on the left. She was short with thick chestnut hair to her shoulders. She was shaking her head, savaging her gag. Her glow was the fiercest and she always fought harder than the others. When you fucked her, her eyes drilled into you like she was willing your skin to catch fire. Sometimes it felt like it did.

Standing at the wall in front of us was Lucy. She was tall and athletic with long black hair and narrow blue eyes. Lucy had been down here the longest. She regarded us coldly, testing her chains, planning her escape. For all her aloofness Lucy pretended to be a passionate zed. Sometimes you thought that it would have been all right to take off her gag and fuck her mouth to mouth, though you never really thought about it seriously.

Kaylan was chained to the wall on the right, the most voluptuous of our zeds. She was the youngest too, about nineteen was our best guess. Her hair shone like spun gold under the lights as she heaved at her chains, eyes flicking everywhere, not sure what was going on.

We stood in the middle of the basement, our naked zeds around us, the intensity of their glow a beacon of desire. Laura let go of my hand and rubbed the goosebumps from her arms. I knew how she felt. It didn't matter how often I'd been down here, it was always vivid, it was always spooky. The zeds were glaring at us, waiting. Marian growled from the back of her throat. I heard Laura swallow.

The door banged open and we all jumped. Mina

started filming Cassie walking down the steps in patent boots, squeezed into a pink rubber corset with a latex G-string, a shiny pointed mask over her eyes. The whizz rush doubled as she glanced at Mina's camera then approached Kaylan. The zed tried to attack but the chains held her in place. Cassie rubbed herself against her and bit her neck, digging fingernails the colour of blood into the zed's tits, licking the front of her gag before moving on.

Cassie worked on Lucy for a few minutes, the zed raising her head and closing her eyes as Cassie got busy with clawed fingers, lipstick mouth and her long tongue. Cassie's smile grew wider as she reached Marian. She looked at the zed, hands on her hips, then she slapped Marian very hard across the face. The zed went wild, flailing against the chains, her body thrashing against the wall. Cassie slapped her harder again, the sharp crack making me wince. Cassie grabbed the zed and pushed her tits into Marian's face, the zed's jaw working viciously behind her gag, desperate to rip and tear, Cassie shaking her shoulders and laughing. She thrust her fingers into Marian's hair and slammed the zed's head against the wall three times, then she snarled and fell on the zed, biting her gag like a zed herself, leaving teethmarks in the rubber.

This drove Marian into a frenzy so Cassie was forced to turn her around and put a hand around her throat, squeezing. She put her other hand on the zed's ass and slid her fingers inside. Choking was the only sure way to calm Marian down, though it didn't work on our other zeds. As Cassie continued to squeeze the zed's movements slowed, her head falling back between her shoulders, legs widening, pressing herself against the wall. Cassie left her and moved quickly to Laura, taking off her dress, pulling down her underwear and leading her over to Kaylan. Cassie slackened the chains and pushed Kaylan to the floor, opening her legs. Laura was kneeling on the carpet, even her pale skin looking tanned next to the zed's.

The iciness of a zed's cunt quickly numbed your tongue. It didn't take long for the cold to creep throughout your face and flutter across your shoulders and down your back in feathery shivers, whizz intensifying this a hundredfold. It was a wonderful, addictive sensation. Laura found this out first hand when Cassie guided her head down between the zed's legs. Laura was unsure at first but it wasn't long before she began to writhe and clutch Kaylan's thighs, forcing them further apart. Laura made a muffled moan as we watched the goosebumps flow down her spine. The zed wrapped her legs around Laura's shoulders and rattled her chains. Cassie left Laura to it and walked towards us. "Now, boys," she said, her eyes voracious behind her mask, "I want you to…"

Chapter 4

Mina hadn't wanted to stay any longer in her parents' house so we'd taken her away on the bikes. We were searching for people, for food, for weapons, for a place to stay. The zeds were everywhere, wearing us down. That night we'd stayed underground in a sewer. We held each other to keep warm and to feel brave, whispering in the dark. Even the stink and the dying rats were better company than the zeds. Sometimes we heard them on the street above, wailing, searching for us. Needless to say, we didn't sleep well.

At what we thought was dawn Cassie crawled up the ladder and took a peep at the world outside. She motioned us to follow. By the time we'd got used to the brightness the zeds were almost on us. We jumped on the bikes, Mina riding behind Cassie. The three of us buzzed away with the disappointed zeds clutching at our heels. The plan had been to ride out of the City to find somewhere safe. The petrol pumps had still been working so fuel wasn't a problem. The terror and despair I'd felt at the church had been momentarily washed away. I had new companions, new friends who'd shown me that the zeds could be killed, and I was already more than halfway in love with Cassie, as was Mina, though I hadn't known it then.

We filled up at one of the petrol stations while I kept the zeds away with the bat. It was looking a little worse for wear, as were we. After days of terror and a night in the sewer we didn't look much better than messy zeds ourselves, and we smelled a lot worse. We wanted to run into the shop to snatch some food but it would have been too dangerous so we rode on, seeing that at last the zeds were beginning to thin out. Now there were only six or seven in view at all times. The worst were the little zeds, the children. It wasn't easy bringing yourself to kill them, making them the most dangerous zeds of all.

After another hour of riding we'd left the City behind. Hills and trees rose around us, lifting our hearts. We rode slowly around the traffic, still unsure on the new bikes. Zeds littered the road and reached for us with shining hands. We passed them by without a glance. It wasn't very long before we began to hear gunshots. They seemed to be coming from somewhere further down the road. We quickened our pace, eager for company, especially the company of those who carried guns.

Within a few minutes we saw someone approaching between the cars. This person, unbelievable as it seemed, appeared to be riding a fucking *pushbike*. We hit the brakes and came to a stop in the middle of the road. Pedalling the bike was a boy in blue shorts and a Superman T-shirt. A rifle and a rucksack were strapped to his back. He skidded to a stop and let his bike fall to the ground. Without a word he unslung his rifle and shot two zeds that had been moving in behind us. He scanned the area, searching for more. When he was satisfied that we were alone he walked up to us, smiling pleasantly.

"I'm heading for the City," he said. "I know that things can't be very pretty there at the moment or you three wouldn't be in such a hurry to leave, but believe me, the City's the place to head for. I've always wanted to live there, and there'll be easier access to food, water and weapons."

The three of us said nothing, we just stared.

"What I'm really looking for," said the boy, "is a nice big house with an even bigger wall around it. That should be quite safe, and there'll be plenty of houses like that around the City, don't you think? I certainly hope so. You're the first people I've seen in fifteen days, it's quite a relief. So, what about you? Can you speak? What are you planning to do? Do you have any weapons? Food? Water? Are you friendly? I'm sorry to say it, but you all smell like a sewer."

It was still dark and Mina was lying beside me in bed, both of us looking at the sky through the window, watching for shooting stars. It was getting chilly but the downers had a hold on me and I was too lethargic to gather the sheets from the floor. I moved closer to Mina instead, stealing her heat. "There's one," she said, pointing, but I didn't see anything. "I'll tell you one of the things I miss the most," continued Mina, her hands crossed behind her head. "Fish."

I was puzzled. "What, cod and tuna, things like that?"

Mina sighed. "No, silly, not fish to eat. Fish to look at. We had an aquarium in our house, a big one. We had six fish. Two of them stuck to the bottom, swimming in the caves and plants. They were the longest ones, catfish or something, I can't remember anymore. The others were more interesting. The funniest was Oscar, he was bigger than your hands. I used to put my head up to the glass and make faces at him like this." Mina waggled her head back and forth, goggle-eyed, cheeks sucked in, mouth open. "Oscar always did the same thing right back. Oscar had personality. He wasn't my favourite fish, though. My favourite was the smallest one, only two inches. It was black, and had a red flash at the end of its tail. It was so small, the other fish should have eaten it, but they never did."

I turned to Mina. "Why not?"

"Because it was a shark," she said, "and other fish don't eat sharks, no matter how small they are."

Mina reached onto the floor and pulled the sheets up, covering us both. We clung to each other and I drifted in and out of consciousness for a few minutes, unable to tell which was which. The last thing I saw before oblivion claimed me was Mina's face in the darkness, the glimmer of her eyes still watching the sky.

The sun woke me up a couple of hours too soon. I rolled out of bed, leaving Mina asleep. I drifted about, washing, eating, making coffee, before making my way into the garden. Kyle was pushing Chloe on the swing, both of them laughing and stealing kisses. I sat next to Bradley and sipped my coffee. He put down his book and looked at me with his grave, sharp features. I lit a cigarette, thinking it might annoy him.

"The military should have intervened earlier," Bradley told me, "but they left it too late. I think that's where most of the people are now; around army barracks, air bases and bunkers. They've probably created *safe zones* or *green areas* around these places. There'll be more people there than you think, thousands of them under martial law, living behind fences. If we picked up a good radio we could speak to a few of them. If we did that they'd come and fetch us in a green truck, they'd take us away to protect us from the zeds. They'd never believe we could survive for long out here in the wild, although I think we can.

"They'd take away our decision making capabilities. No drink, no drugs, no cigarettes, definitely no sexual activity, deviant or otherwise. Except for the girls of course, who'd be used as prostitutes for the squaddies. You certainly wouldn't find life such fun."

This was way too disturbing to deal with first thing in the morning. "Bradley, why are you telling me this?"

"I'm telling you this to make you understand that the

63

zeds aren't our only enemies. Now listen to me. If you ever hear a gunshot, or see a truck, or a car, anything of that nature, don't run towards them with open arms. *Stay away*. No one else will understand the life we lead here. They'll think it's wrong."

"What about you?" I said. "You're a saint, you wouldn't miss any of the things we do."

"That's true," nodded Bradley, "but here I have a position of responsibility. I'm the mechanic, I'm in charge of weapons and supplies; food, water, petrol. Do you really think that a bunch of soldiers will give me a post like that? They'd sit me in a corner and wait for me to grow another six inches before even thinking about taking me seriously.

"I like it here, and I want to stay. Please explain what I've said to the others, it's very important that you make them understand, especially Cassandra. You'll know they've got the message when they start to look frightened, just like you do now." Bradley looked at me for a few more seconds before picking up his book and disappearing again under his hat.

No one had much trouble accepting Bradley's theory. We all agreed to shun the possibility of contact with others. We didn't want the harmony of our house destroyed. After sealing the bargain with gin and tonics we sat down to watch more movies.

The shotgun boomed and our rifles cracked. Food had exploded everywhere, the stench of curdled milk and rotten eggs making us gag. There were way too many zeds coming in from every direction, they were even clambering over the fucking shelves. I was nearly deaf from the gunfire, nearly blind with all the smoke, nearly dead from the fear. If it wasn't for the whizz keeping me on line I think I'd just have dropped to my knees and waited for the end.

The five of us were trapped in a dark corner of the supermarket and the space between us and the zeds was diminishing all too quickly. Mina ran out of bullets and had to reload, then Kyle ran out of shells and was left with his pistol. Time was running out. The shelves began collapsing under the weight of the eager zeds. The surrounding pile of bodies was over three feet high, not that it made much difference, there were still plenty of zeds for everybody. One of us needed to come up with a plan but there just wasn't time to think. We pressed our backs to the wall and continued to shoot.

The zeds were two metres away, a solid wall of glowing skin and ragged clothes. This time when our guns ran out there'd be no time to reload. I saw Bradley take something from his back pocket. The thought flashed through my mind that it was a hand grenade and he was going to blow us all to hell. Instead he pointed the thing at the zeds, spraying them. Lighter fuel. Under the gunfire they went up like torches and in no time at all the place was an inferno. Great, I thought, instead of getting ripped apart we were going to burn to death.

As we started to cook, Bradley grabbed a bottle of water from the trolley and doused himself. The rest of us got the idea and copied him. Bradley leapt through the flames with the four of us close behind. We sprinted down the burning aisle, past the thrashing zeds until we reached the windows, which we blew out with the last of our bullets. We jumped out into the car park, the clear air like heaven. Burning zeds followed us from the supermarket, clothes gone, flesh melting down to bone. Cassie and Chloe shot them impassively while we climbed into the jeep. The two girls waited for a few seconds before ducking inside. Chloe gunned the engine and drove us sedately away.

"You didn't get any food, then," said Cassie.

"No, I'm sorry," said Bradley, blackened and soaked as we all were. "We ran into some trouble. There was a rush for the barbecue sale and things got out of hand, you know how pushy some people can get."

That night we drank as much vodka as we could, ice cold from the freezer. The worst injuries we'd suffered were singed eyebrows. Everyone's respect for Bradley had grown again, not that he would have any of it. He hated praise, it embarrassed him. Chloe took the bottle around again, refilling our glasses. Mina turned Frank Sinatra up and started to dance with Kyle. I was on the couch between Laura and Cassie, senses detaching themselves from my body. It took a great deal of concentrated willpower to tip some more vodka down my throat. I wondered idly if I was going to be sick. It didn't seem to matter.

I arose from unconsciousness with a nauseating lurch. My tongue was a withered prune in the desert. I found myself hanging off the edge of the bed, pushed there by Cassie, Mina and Laura, who were all still asleep. Kyle was wrapped in a foetal position in the corner beneath the window. I groaned like a zed and wished I'd died in the supermarket fire. Laura gave me a final push and I spilled from the bed and hit the floor hard, fully expecting my brains to burst out from my eyesockets. I cried out for help but no one could hear me. I was going to die alone.

By noon everyone was feeling a little better. Laura had stopped throwing up and we'd cleaned up the vomit from the night before off the carpets. I choked down some soup and a piece of bread. I thought I might feel well enough for a cigarette so I smoked one in the garden with a mug of tea, Mina sitting pale beside me, massaging her temples, staring at the grass.

Snatches of memory about last night were beginning to come back. Chloe falling asleep on the couch with her hands covering her eyes. Kyle gulping from the bottle, spilling vodka over his face, the rest of us laughing. Trying to fuck Cassie on the couch and failing, the sound of her taunts, trying to walk using legs that had turned to jelly. Mina being sick, followed by me. A long journey to the bedroom, eyes pointing in different directions. The cool sheets on the mattress.

Laura, Mina and Chloe were asleep before ten. I sat chewing peanuts on the couch with Cassie and Kyle. I was still fragile but well over the worst of it. We popped some downers, washing the pills down with what little water we had remaining. We'd have to shopping again tomorrow, hopefully this time with more success. The day before had been too close, the nearest I'd come to losing it since I'd first met Cassie. If it hadn't been for Bradley then everything would have been over. We'd have joined the zeds, the shining ones.

The front door being shut woke us up before dawn. We complained to each other and stretched, stiff from the couch. Kyle muttered something, wiping drool from his cheek while I stood up and yawned. Bradley strode into the room and greeted us brightly. "Don't you all look attractive," he said. "Another hard night's hedonism? Love those bags under your eyes, Cassandra. While you've been snoring at each other I've been out foraging. I've collected some more ammunition for our weapons and I saw a zed walk off the top of a high building. Was it suicide or merely stupidity? Who can tell? I also found this. What do you think?" Bradley showed us a flashy looking machine gun and beamed. Kyle yawned and Cassie shook out her hair. "I'm overwhelmed," said Bradley, smile fading.

"Perhaps you'll be more responsive this afternoon."

This time the shopping expedition went without a hitch. Plenty of water, food and alcohol. More cigarettes, lots of crisps and chocolate along with powdered milk. There hadn't been too many zeds around. Bradley enjoyed his new machine gun but he'd had problems holding it steady. We loaded the jeep in the zed car park as some rain began to fall. Kyle complained of how he missed the weather forecasts. "It's all so unpredictable now," he said. Cassie put another zed down and we were off.

"What's the plan for tonight?" I asked, squeezed with the others in the back of the jeep.

"Whizz!" cried Cassie and Mina in unison.

"As long as it isn't vodka," said Laura.

"We don't have any left," put in Kyle, watching the street pass through the window. "Look at that fucking zed, Alex. Can you believe it? It's wearing its guts as a hat! Where's the sense in that?"

"Zed fashion," said Bradley sagely. "Living death, intestines and cannibalism are all the rage this season. Don't you notice it when you walk down the highstreet? I've never seen anything catch on so quickly. Look at that one for instance. It's very chic to have your cheeks ripped open in that particular style. It accentuates the sensuous line of the jawbone and creates that pleasing flap effect, rather like the gills of a fish. Would you consider something along those lines for yourself, Chloe?"

"I like my cheeks as they are, thanks."

"Shame, you have the structure for it."

Suddenly Kyle jumped and banged his head on the roof. "Wait! Stop! Back up. Wait here, I won't be long." Kyle opened the door and left the jeep, paying no attention to our insults. He walked up to a vacuous looking teenage zed with the flesh ripped from his back. This zed was stumbling past a burnt out café with shattered windows. Other zeds began converging, too many to shoot down. Kyle took out his pistol and stood in the path of the vacuous zed. He smiled, entire face lighting up, then he shot the zed through the mouth.

"Sorry about that," said Kyle, getting back in the jeep and slamming the door. "It was someone I used to know. I always hated that fucker. Shame he didn't recognise me but you can't have everything. What are you looking at me like that for? You people need to lighten up."

The whizz flew up my nose with a burn and a sting. The rain had become heavier outside and the wind had picked up, whistling at the window. Bradley was editing Cassie's basement movie while the rest of us scattered ourselves around the living room. Kyle had ripped his shirt off and was doing press-ups in front of the TV, responding to Chloe's claim that he could do with better muscle definition. I grabbed Cassie and ran around the room with her, jumping over the grunting Kyle, hurdling the coffee table, dodging around the couch and finally crashing into a chair, sprawling at Laura's bare feet. I clutched her ankles and pulled her down on top of me. Chloe, Cassie and Mina had formed a ring around Kyle, taunting him. I kissed Laura and she attacked my back with her nails, a live wire in my arms. She sank her teeth into my shoulder as I reached for the open wrap on the table. We licked some whizz up and kissed again, our spit bitter but beautiful.

Laura jumped up and ran out of the room with me close behind. She opened the front door and disappeared into the darkness. When I followed she was nowhere to be seen. Within seconds I was soaked, the wind whipping the rain in my face, the trees rattling and creaking above me. I ran to the side of the house then around the back. Laura was waiting there, her clothes gone, hair plastered to her skin. The only light came murky from the house. I lost my clothes and we joined, cold as zeds. We fucked in the grass and the rain, Laura's cries echoing around us, flying as high as the clouds.

Towels, bathrobes and whisky dried us off and warmed us up. We sat together on the floor with a cigarette each, Laura adjusting the towel that was wrapped around her hair. Kyle claimed that he'd pulled a muscle on his fifty-fourth press-up. He rotated his shoulder and winced theatrically. Cassie offered him a massage but he flatly refused. "It just needs rest," he said. "Don't worry about me." Kyle scowled before stalking off to his room.

At dawn the clouds began to clear and by the afternoon it was hot and sunny. Refreshed by four hours of sleep, we were ready for some exploring. Kyle's shoulder had healed quickly and he was happy to come along but Chloe wouldn't be persuaded. "I don't like motorbikes," was the only thing she'd say.

After bombing some extra whizz to keep us frosty we tooled up and set off. We headed out of the City, riding north this time where we'd rarely been before. It all looked the same, though; miles of empty cars and a parade of zeds. We stopped to slice a few and Cassie took some Polaroids. Laura couldn't remember her score anymore, either, guessing about one hundred and fifty.

We didn't have time to smoke as the zeds had got wind of us and were multiplying fast. We rode a few more miles down the road, passing an enormous shopping complex where there had to be a thousand zeds at least, just milling around in the car park. The whizz was biting hard and the houses were thinning out fast. We were back in the countryside again, the road cutting through it like a cement blade. On the clearest stretch we stopped to have our long-awaited cigarettes. Mina shot the only zeds in sight, two women and a teenage boy. One of the women looked promising until I saw the wounds on her legs. Impure.

Cassie thought that her basement movie would be ready soon. I had to admit to myself that I wasn't looking forward to seeing it. From the looks on Laura's and Kyle's faces I thought that they were feeling the same way. We just weren't performers like Cassie. I didn't know about Mina. She was sitting back to back with Cassie on the roof of a car. Maybe she was thinking about tiny sharks.

I lay down flat on the road and gazed at the sky, enjoying the surge of whizz and sucking up the silence that I'd never experienced until the zeds came. Laura and Kyle were standing alert on zed patrol. Cassie had been right about Laura all along, she was really opening out. It just took a little time. She'd fucked Mina for the first time last week, which had to be a good sign, though Cassie thought she was still too passive. When Laura saw me watching her she pointed her pistol at me and raised her eyebrows until I looked away.

"We should get going soon," Kyle said, pacing the road.

"You shouldn't be so jumpy," Cassie told him.

"I'm not jumpy."

"You're jumping like a bean. Is it your shoulder?"

"My shoulder's fine," said Kyle testily.

"That's not how it looked last night. You should have let me massage it, I'm good. My mother taught me. What do you think of my massages, Mina?"

"Fantastic," Mina said.

"There you go." Cassie threw her cigarette onto the road not far from Kyle's feet. "It's your loss," she said. Kyle turned away and Cassie smiled, not kindly. "Who was that dumb looking zed you put down yesterday? School bully?"

71

"School dealer," said Kyle. "*I* was the school bully."

"That's nice." Cassie was still smiling. "So how come you don't bully me, Kyle? Some girls like a firm hand." Mina began to laugh. Laura was looking away, rubbing her arm.

"Sorry," said Kyle, "I'm retired." He saw a zed in the distance and shot at it but the zed was out of range.

One by one the girls drifted away to bed until there were just the two of us left. I lay further back on the armchair, spreading my ass with my hands so Kyle could fuck me deeper. He sank in all the way, his weight pressing me back into the cushions, hand squeezing my dick. I closed my eyes, legs high and wide, and Kyle pulled back then pushed in hard, coming inside me with a moan. He moved in and out one last time then slid out of me quickly, making me wince. I opened my eyes and saw Bradley standing in the doorway, looking sceptical. "I'm seeing more parallels between you and your famous namesake all the time," he said.

Leaving his clothes on the floor, Kyle blundered to his room, pushing past Bradley and slamming the door. Bradley took some water from the kitchen then went back to the library. I stayed on the chair for a few minutes, trying to get my breath back. The house was silent, which didn't happen often. We liked being noisy to make up for the silence outside. I wanted to go to bed but I needed to come first so I picked up the tube of KY and moved naked into the kitchen, taking the torch from the cupboard. The nerves began stealing over me as I opened the door to the basement. I flicked on the torch and stepped through the door. I walked down the steps with my heart hammering in my ears.

The basement was spooky enough under the lights, surrounded by music and friends. Alone in the dark it was something else altogether. I turned off the torch and dropped it to the floor, waiting in the middle of the room. The shining zeds stood like imprisoned angels around me, filling the basement with their glow. The chains clinked and I shivered, not really knowing what I was doing alone down here. Kaylan gave a haunted moan. The zeds waited impassively, the glitter of their eyes slicing into me, making me hard, drawing me to Lucy.

She turned her head away as I walked towards her. I ran my hands through her silken zed hair and over her sides, hypnotised by the glow of Lucy's skin and the shadow of my hands as they passed over her. The zed looked at me as I moved closer until we were eyeball to eyeball. I squeezed some KY onto my fingers and pushed them into the zed then I fucked her against the wall, frozen in her milky cunt, biting on her pearl of a nipple. Lucy continued to stare, eyes flat and hard as jewels, running her icy foot up the back of my leg then jumping on me suddenly and wrapping her legs around me. I sucked on her gag, losing myself in her zed glance and putting my wrists over her hands. She clutched them tight, chaining me to her as she was chained, flooding me with cold.

I came with a sting and struggled to get free but my orgasm had made me weak and Lucy wouldn't let go. I sagged against her, burying my face in her hair until she released me. I looked up at the zed from the floor but Lucy had grown perfectly still again, staring at nothing, my come trailing down her leg. When I went back upstairs I crawled into bed between Cassie and Mina, their warm bodies healing me, thawing me out. Mina mumbled something and turned over. I put an arm around Cassie and thought about the zeds below us, waiting in the dark.

The afternoon was hazy and hot. We drank tequila in the garden, Cassie, Kyle and Mina deepening their tans, the rest of us hiding in the shade. The heat and the alcohol had wrapped me in a foggy, dream-like state. I grinned at Laura and planted a kiss on her cheek. She laughed, keeping her eyes on Cassie, who was dressed only in her sunglasses.

"What about my movie, Bradley?" said Cassie.

Bradley glanced up from his book on fossil fuels. "I'm finding that I'm only able to work on it in short bursts. I don't want to go blind. I'm just surprised that any of you can see at all, especially you, Laura. I'd been under the impression that you were camera-shy."

Cassie lifted her shades. "Laura's a star in the making. Leave her alone."

Bradley held up a hand in surrender and went back to his book. Chloe yawned and refilled her glass, muttering something about a headache. We all heard a zed moving on the street outside, not a pleasant sound. We stayed quiet until it had gone. I followed Laura to the swing and gave her a gentle push while Chloe told the others that we needed to pay another visit to the pharmacy. Our pills were running low.

"I never thought I'd be living in a place like this," Laura said as she swung. "I wish I could tell my mum about it."

"She probably wouldn't approve," I said, giving Laura a bigger push.

"Well I wouldn't tell her *everything*, obviously, just some of the stuff." Laura laughed. "I'm not making sense," she said. "Mum's a zed now. So is everyone else. That doesn't bother me so much anymore. Maybe I'll be a zed too one day. Maybe we all will."

I didn't find this possibility appealing but I didn't say anything. "We'll go to the chemist's tomorrow," Chloe told us, pinching the bridge of her nose. "Make a list of everything you need. Christ, this headache's killing me.

Must be the sun."

"I want to go higher," ordered Laura, so I gave her a bigger push and watched her hair fly.

"Careful on that swing," ordered Mina with her hand shading her eyes.

Laura laughed and pointed her toes, ankle bracelet sparkling. "Live fast, die young," she said as she rushed through the air, "leave an animated corpse." We all laughed and I stopped pushing Laura to have another drink and a cigarette.

Cassie came to bed with me early that night. She wanted to fuck but I was too drunk. I was watching the room twist around me, Cassie's hand on my chest keeping me steady. "I'll need to get some dye in the chemist's tomorrow," she said. "Mina needs some as well, her roots are showing, have you noticed?" Cassie kissed my nipple then bit it sharply, hurting me. The bedroom door opened and Mina came in wearing blue pyjamas. She jumped onto the bed, laughing at my complaints. I turned to face the wall, letting my eyes close. Mina started tickling me and I had to grit my teeth. I won through and she eventually gave up. "It's no good," Mina said, "he must be getting old. Your roots are coming through, Cass. Get some dye tomorrow."

The trip turned out to be fun. It was my turn to have the shotgun, always a bonus. Bradley had taken sole possession of the new machine gun but no one minded. I chatted with Laura while Chloe and Bradley searched the district. It took half an hour to find the kind of place we were after, a modern pharmacy that was white and spacious, like you'd think the inside of a spaceship should look.

Chloe, Cassie and Mina shot their way inside as the rest of us watched for the zeds that we knew were out there. This street was long and straight, not giving much cover for any over cautious zeds. Kyle emptied the Uzi into an expensive looking sports car. He wanted it to explode like they did in the movies but it just wouldn't go up. The tyres burst and one of the doors fell off but that was it. Kyle shot a few zeds with his pistol to vent his frustration. Laura spotted a zed on the roof above a chip shop. She brought it down with the rifle and it cracked onto the pavement head first, skull splitting open. "Gross," said Laura, wrinkling her nose. I managed to blow a zed's legs off with the shotgun, drawing some acclaim before Bradley stepped in and shot the writhing zed through the forehead.

"Sadism is the mark of a warped and decadent mind," he informed me.

I racked the shotgun and took a step forward. "Fuck the zeds, they'd kill us all if they could, and they wouldn't be too fussy about how they did it, either. I'm just doing to them what they'd do to me."

"You're missing the point," said Bradley, pausing to shoot another zed. "They have no choice in this matter. We do. Under these circumstances it's easy to fall down to the basest level, you yourself prove that. We should still remain as civilised, as human as we can."

"I *am* human!" I shouted.

"All too human," said Bradley as the girls came back on the street with their baskets and their guns. Chloe was wearing three pairs of shades on her head. Mina had two. We retreated to the jeep, shooting as we went. Cassie was the last one to get inside, waiting to kill four more zeds before sliding onto the seat and banging the door shut.

Chapter 5

Bradley had taken Chloe and Kyle out in the jeep to siphon petrol. Kyle hadn't wanted to go but he was persuaded when Bradley said that he could use the new machine gun. He wouldn't be able to fire it while they were siphoning, of course, but I wasn't so sure that Kyle realised that. The three of them would be back in a few hours, stinking to high heaven. It took days to wash off the smell, making it the most hated job in the house.

The kitchen had been commandeered by Cassie and Mina, who were dyeing their hair. I could make out their voices through the open bedroom door, Mina's voice the higher pitched, Cassie's the louder. Mina had briefly wondered whether she should go for purple but she followed Cassie's advice and decided to stick with black. I thought she should throw in a little bit of red to remind Mina of her favourite shark but I couldn't say anything as I was pinned to the bed by Laura. She'd fallen asleep almost immediately after we'd fucked, a habit of hers when she wasn't whizzing.

"These gloves are shit," Cassie was saying.

"Make sure I don't get any in my eye," said Mina worriedly. "It was bad enough when Kyle came in it."

"No shit," said Cassie. "That wanker nearly ruined my movie! Just how hard can it be to aim in someone's mouth?"

"This stuff always burns my scalp."

"You've got sensitive skin. Stop wriggling, you're just making things worse. That's better."

"It stings! Fuckfuckfuck!"

"Is that all you can think about?"

I laughed to myself and squeezed Laura to me, closing my eyes. Just before falling asleep I heard Mina telling Cassie not to pull her hair so hard, didn't she know that it hurt?

The whizz went around in the night and the gin was beginning to flow. Cassie and Kyle had taken a trip to the basement ten minutes ago. They probably wouldn't be back for a while. An action movie was flashing by on the television screen, something about tiny robots that could get into your brain and control your actions. I sat next to Mina, stroking her glossy new hair, bored by the film that I'd already seen twice before. What I needed was a change of scenery.

The library that Bradley had put together lay at the end of the hallway. I stood at the open door, watching Bradley munch contentedly on a pickle sandwich. Ceiling high bookshelves lined three of the walls. The last wall was dominated by a huge window and an even bigger desk. The editing suite stood on the top, next to a lamp and a modest stereo. A glass of water tinkling with ice stood close to Bradley's hand. Tinny sounding pop music came quietly from the speakers on the floor.

Bradley noticed me standing there and waved me inside, brushing the crumbs from his Professor X T-shirt. I wheeled a black office chair from the corner and joined Bradley, who left his sandwich half eaten on his plate. "You don't come in here very often," he said, looking suspicious. "Did Cassandra send you? I'm working as fast as I can. Why is she so impatient? It's not like she has to go anywhere."

I swivelled on the chair, looking at the array of books. "That's not why I'm here. I'm just being sociable. Smells like petrol in here, and pickles."

"Looking at the way you treat your nose I'm surprised that you can smell anything at all."

"Who's your favourite X-Man?" I asked, but Bradley ignored me. He took a bite from his sandwich and pressed a button. Cassie appeared on the monitor dressed in her rubber corset. The camera followed her to Laura, who was sucking greedily on Kaylan's tits, her hand cupping the zed's cold ass. I glanced at Bradley, who was chewing mildly at the monitor. Now I was on the screen, fucking Marian with a weird expression on my face that I didn't like one bit.

"Editing can be great fun," said Bradley through a mouthful of pickle. "Would you like slow motion on this part? See, it's much more dramatic, don't you think?"

I disagreed, turning away in the chair. Some pictures had been tacked onto the wall next to the window. I'd liked to have known who the people in the pictures were but I was sure that Bradley wouldn't tell me so I didn't ask. Bradley finished his sandwich and pressed some more buttons, at random it seemed to me. I asked him where he kept finding our guns, the whizz making me inquisitive.

"Here, there and everywhere," answered Bradley. "They're not difficult to pick up. Police cars, vans, army trucks or jeeps."

"So why do you go out at night?"

"I prefer the night, I find it safer. Darkness is cover and it makes the zeds easier to spot. You've never shown curiosity before. Why are you asking me this?"

I shrugged. "I don't know. I'm just interested."

"Well, that's good. Put that cigarette away."

Cassie surprised me by appearing in the doorway. She strode in and planted her hands on my shoulders. "I hope you haven't been twisting his mind, Bradley." Cassie spun me a couple of times on the chair and pulled me up with a smile and a kiss. I chased her out Bradley's library and through the hallway into the living room where the movie was just finishing. I caught Cassie as she was dodging past Mina and we fell onto the carpet with Cassie biting me like a zed. We vacuumed up some more whizz, using the same monster line, meeting at the centre where our noses touched.

Within fifteen minutes of first meeting Bradley he'd convinced us of his plan. The three of us agreed to ride back into the City with the strange boy in the superhero T-shirt in an attempt to find a safe place to stay. Bradley had been reluctant to leave his push-bike behind but he hadn't really had much choice. He rode behind me on the motorbike, clutching my sides in a death grip.

We rode aimlessly for hours, the constant zeds numbing me into desolation. I was riding on automatic, everything but the zeds locked out. The rain hadn't had the chance to wash away the blood yet and some streets were swimming in it, the smell cutting through our sewer stink with ease. The roads were endless, the flies were endless, the zeds were endless. What was the point? It was all finished.

The road began to widen out, so did the houses. Cornershops and takeaways had long since disappeared. The cars strewn over the road had become flashier. We rode up a long hill, then past a park where little zeds were swarming. "We might be getting close to what we're after," Bradley said in my ear. "Keep at it." The road wound left in a slow curve then went downhill again. Before very long a pretentious sign told us that we were entering Hemdale Gardens. When we saw a zed wearing a tuxedo and a tacky yellow Ferrari that had crashed into an Aston Martin we knew we were in the right kind of place.

Within another hour we'd found the house that offered the best protection; number twenty-two. The zeds began converging as we boosted Bradley up and over the gate. He made it with a scramble and disappeared over the top. We hopped about until the gate slid open then we ran inside, slamming the gate shut in the faces of the zeds. After wading through the garden we reached the house, not as huge as I'd imagined considering the size of the walls around it. Bradley warned us about alarms but when we broke in there wasn't a sound.

"What happens next?" Mina asked us.

"We search the place for zeds," Cassie said, hefting the baseball bat.

Bradley was confused. "Zeds?"

It was getting dark by the time we were satisfied that the place was clean. The search itself had been agonising. I was wound up so tight I thought I'd snap in two. Every room, every wardrobe, behind the furniture, under the beds, around the garage, into the basement, up to the attic, out on the balcony, and all of it empty. Apart from us.

The four of us spent most of the night in the huge bath, tub after tub, washing away the filth and the grime. We dressed in fluffy bathrobes and looted the kitchen, making the biggest meal we could find with Mina as head chef. After that it was time to raid the drinks cabinet and the wine rack, drowning ourselves in alcohol while Bradley stuck to water, checking the television to see if anyone was still broadcasting. The only CDs around were classical; Mozart, Brahms and Schoenberg. We listened to the orchestras together on the couch, crying, drinking, stunned to be alive. Eventually the stereo switched itself off and we went to bed.

Bradley was the only one who wanted to sleep alone. The rest of us found the biggest bed in the house and tumbled into it with Cassie in the middle. I passed out after a few minutes but I was woken up at three twenty-six by Cassie's kisses. She climbed on top of me and we fucked as Mina snored gently beside us. She soon woke up and ran a tentative hand over Cassie's tits. Mina moaned when Cassie grabbed her hair and kissed her hard on the mouth. I came very quickly after that.

On September the second I turned sixteen. The party started at midnight with gin and tonics and tremendous amounts of whizz. Everyone (even Bradley) sung Happy Birthday and lined up with their presents. From Chloe I had a vibrating mobile phone, Kyle gave me a copy of The Return Of The Living Dead, Mina gave me a Darth Vader helmet and a giant cup and saucer, and Laura gave me an ugly but chunky gold watch. From Cassie I had an inflatable sex doll, a hideous snakeskin jacket, a huge carved dragon and a rubber hand that could crawl along the floor. Bradley needed Kyle's help to carry his present into the living room, a long wooden box that they lowered carefully onto the carpet. I opened it with trepidation. Inside I found a sea of Styrofoam which I quickly cleared away.

"What's this?" I asked, confused by what I was seeing.

"It's a rocket launcher," answered Bradley proudly.

It took us nearly half an hour to set the launcher up on the balcony but at last it was sitting on its little tripod, loaded and ready to fire. I excitedly lowered myself on one knee and settled a shoulder beneath it. "I can't see anything," I complained, squinting through the sight. Bradley flicked a switch close to my ear. There was a hum and suddenly my vision was flooded with a sea of green. There was our wall, the road and the house opposite which just had to be my target.

"Press this first," said Bradley over the chatter of the others, "then this. All you have to do then is fire the thing. Everyone stand back."

I pressed the buttons Bradley had told me to, took a few deep anticipatory breaths, then I fired. There was a whooshing sound and the rocket careered away, zipping over the street before annihilating the front of our neighbour's house in a truly majestic explosion.

"Thanks, Bradley," I said, quite choked up about the whole thing. "Thank you everyone, this is a great birthday." They all cheered and we ran downstairs to get on with the party.

Twenty hours later Cassie took me down into the basement. I couldn't help laughing when I saw the zeds. Cassie had put paper hats on their heads and tied streamers around their chains. Marian's hat had slipped over one eye, making her the cutest zed I'd ever seen. A gaudy sign had been pinned onto the wall; "Happy Birthday Alex, from your loving zeds, Marian, Kaylan and Lucy, xxx."

I watched the sun rise with Chloe and Kyle, sharing another bottle of wine. The damage on the opposite house was undeniably impressive. We talked about what we'd lost and what we'd gained until the bottle was empty and we all felt like crying. I went back inside and cleaned my teeth, reflecting on the party, feeling tired, drunk and happy. When I opened the bedroom door I found Cassie, Mina and Laura, all of them smiling and naked apart from the huge pink satin bows that were tied around their waists. My sixteenth was without a shadow of a doubt the best birthday I'd ever had.

Casablanca had just finished and Bradley was crying again. Cassie put the DVD player on to watch pornography while Chloe put some music on. Kyle finished his beer and crushed the can, giving me a strange look before he turned to Chloe. "We need some new films," he said. "Will you take us to the videostore tomorrow?"

"Only if you cover me when I stop for some new shoes." Chloe looked sadly at her feet. "I'm tired of the ones I've got."

"Count me in," said Laura, "only I need a dress as well."

"I think this is getting out of hand," said Kyle.

"Tough." Chloe smiled and kissed the tip of Kyle's nose.

"I need some boots too," said Laura. "What do you think, Cassie?"

"Hmm mm," Cassie said, watching the screen.

"What's this about boots?" asked Mina, coming into the room with a magazine in her hand. She smiled at me then tugged Laura's hair.

"Movies and clothes," I said. "We're running low."

Mina nodded and sat on the arm of Cassie's chair. "I'm glad you like the helmet," she said to me.

"It's a fucking improvement," noted Kyle.

"Masks upon masks," said Bradley, wiping his nose with a tissue.

We were off the following afternoon, all seven of us crammed into the jeep, whizzing and ready for anything. Chloe rolled us out of the garage, down the driveway and through the gate. A particularly messy zed in a swimsuit watched us drive past as we headed for the shops. I told Mina about the red flash I thought she should put in her hair. She said that she'd think about it, but I didn't hold out much hope.

The video store was first on the list. Kyle, Bradley and Cassie had gone inside through the open doors. The zeds weren't causing much of a problem and within ten minutes we were all back in the jeep, driving away and chattering about our new film collection. Kyle had picked up the action movies and some sci-fi, Cassie went for the slasher films and some soft porn while Bradley had grabbed all the Bogart movies he could carry.

Next was the shoe shop. The ruined street was more crowded here and we had to work hard to keep the zeds at a safe distance. The girls ran out of the shop and loaded up before disappearing inside again. The zeds kept falling and I wondered idly to myself about the possible long term damage being done to our ears by all the gunfire. Bradley was cutting a swathe with his new machine gun to my right. Kyle stood behind us brandishing the shotgun and shouting insults at the zeds.

The sky had been clogging up all day and it was beginning to spit with rain as the girls left the shop for the last time. We stopped firing and hurried to the jeep which was filling with the smell of new leather. Chloe switched on the wipers and knocked over some stray zeds while I asked Laura if she'd found any boots.

"Lots," she answered happily, "but I don't have anything to go with them. Not yet, anyway."

The clothes shop was a tricky proposition. We may not have been in the City Centre but we were getting closer all the time. The shop the girls wanted to break into was on Quigley Street, which we'd just discovered was crawling with zeds. Bradley advised turning back but the girls shouted him down. Chloe crashed through a few zeds before stopping outside the shop. We leapt onto the street and started shooting. The zeds quickly surrounded us to move in for the kill. I saw one pure-looking zed I wouldn't have minded fucking but this wasn't really the time or the place. The zed went down with the others.

It took us fifteen minutes to clear enough space for the girls to get into the shop. I was standing on guard with Bradley and Kyle. The zeds didn't stop coming but their numbers weren't threatening anymore. I heard some pistol shots coming from somewhere inside the shop, three, four, five. After dropping another zed I saw an army truck turn out of a side street and start moving towards us. I gaped at it, everything Bradley had told me flying around my mind, bursting my bubble, making me feel caught.

"Move!" yelled Bradley. "The shop!" He ran inside, followed by Kyle. I was moving in slow motion, heading for the door, risking a stupid glance behind me, seeing a slim gun barrel poking from the truck's window and a red dot from a laser sight marking my side. I stopped and dropped my rifle, glancing in the shop window, motioning for Bradley to go deeper inside. He saw the laser spot, nodded, and disappeared. Three men jumped out from the back of the truck and came for me, the rifle still as a rock from the passenger window. The men were wearing army fatigues, one of them with sunglasses pushed back on his head. All of them were smiling with pistols in their hands.

I'd been bundled into the truck and we'd been driving for around twenty minutes. I was terrified but cogent, glad that the others had got away. My captors hadn't said a word, they just laughed every now and then, sucking on reefers while I rolled about the metal floor, struggling against the ropes that held me. The truck stopped and I heard two doors slamming. I tried rolling over to see what was happening but someone booted me in the back to keep me where I was. I stayed and waited, hearing someone new climb into the truck. There was some low muttering, a crazy giggle that stopped my breath, then a knife cut the T-shirt from my back. This was not happening to me. My feet were untied and the rest of my clothes hauled off me. Hairy hands flipped me over onto my back.

A green man was standing there, stubby dick in his hand, the name Walters printed on his shirt. He was flanked by two others, a fat man wearing the shades and the crazy giggler, bald and bearded. He giggled again and I

86

tried to say something tough but my voice wasn't working and I could only croak. Gunshots came from somewhere outside. For a second I thought it was Cassie and the rest but then I realised that the other army men were keeping the zeds away. Walters nodded and made a sign with his hand. The fat man turned me onto my stomach then someone stuck a jellied finger up my ass, feeling around, lubricating me.

Walters called me a good boy before his weight pressed me to the floor. I gritted my teeth and tried to think good thoughts while Walters fumbled around my ass and pushed his dick into me, blowing in my ear with cannabis breath. I tried to picture Cassie or Kyle but my mind wasn't working, I couldn't fucking see them, and without knowing it at first I started to cry. The crazy giggler took over when Walters was done, his dick much bigger, splitting me in two. I cried out and Walters appeared by my head, pushing his dick in my face, telling me to suck it. I imagined biting it off and spitting the fucking thing at him, but I didn't.

As the giggler came he licked my neck and bit my shoulder hard. He climbed off me and the fat man crushed me to the floor. He'd even kept his shades on. He started fucking me, wheezing as I heard more gunshots, choking on Walters's dick with a raging fire in my ass. The only things I could taste were smegma and lubricant. Someone shouted before I heard a volley from a machine gun. The fat man rolled off me and Walters pulled away. I threw up over the floor, turning to see the crazy giggler collapsing with his head blown open. Four figures jumped into the truck and the fat man went for a pistol, getting shot in the face and falling into the pool of my vomit. Cassie charged Walters with a roar and kicked him squarely in the balls with her big trainer. Chloe folded me into her arms and I watched Cassie, Mina and Laura stamping on Walters's face, kicking some teeth out of his mouth and knocking him unconscious.

During the journey home I kept my eyes down, trying not to think. No one spoke. When we reached the house I went straight inside, leaving the others to unload the jeep. I washed myself three times then popped a couple of downers with a glass of whisky, then another. Slowly I was beginning to unfreeze. I smoked a cigarette in the bedroom, stomach erupting in rage and love for the girls, my avengers. I heard the others moving through the house, whispering to each other and dragging something along with them. Eventually Cassie came in to see me. She took me by the shoulders and kissed my forehead, saying that she loved me, which she'd only told me once before. I followed her through the hallway and into the kitchen where the basement door was standing open.

"This will make you feel better," Cassie said.

Laura and Kyle were sitting low on the basement steps. They looked at me as I sat down above them, watching Cassie reach the floor where Mina was waiting with folded arms. The girls' feet crackled over the plastic sheeting that was laid over the carpet. Our zeds were quiet, all of them gazing at Walters, who was tied up naked on the floor with a zed gag over his mouth, his eyes rolling wildly. Bruises were already forming over his ribs and his nose was broken, running freely with mucus and blood. Cassie glanced at me and removed the gag. Walters began choking then coughed out a thick wad of blood over the plastic. I think there might have been a tooth in there as well.

"Look, you kids," Walters began, "you have to let me go, this isn't some fucking game here. You! Little girl! Untie me, that's all you have to do. Don't fuck around with me here." Walters looked at the zeds who were chained to the wall before turning back to the impassive Cassie. "Who's in charge here? Who has authority? Let me see them. What about parents? Who takes care of you? Just let me fucking see them, I need to talk to someone. Listen to me, girl, what do you think you're doing? Don't touch that fucking chain, leave it alone and we'll talk, what the fuck *is* this? Look, you can't do this, you're only children, you can't make this kind of decision! Let me go!"

The zeds were moving in towards Walters, Marian in the lead. Cassie slipped off their gags and moved quickly away. As Walters began to plead with us Mina put a disc on the stereo, making me laugh when I heard the song. It was Frank, singing 'Too Close For Comfort'. Walters's pleas turned to screams as the zeds came closer. He was struggling valiantly with the ropes but it didn't do any good. Marian reached him first, very beautiful without her gag.

"You shouldn't have fucked with him," said Cassie as Marian fell on Walters, tearing a hole in his face. Our other two zeds found him and got to work. Walters's screams rose in pitch until he sounded like a child. Within a minute the floor was running with blood and Walters was ripped open from balls to neck, the zeds moving over him silently, intestines wrapped around their arms like pulsing bracelets.

I lit a cigarette, surprised and pleased to see that Walters was still alive. Most of his face was covered in blood, which made it difficult to read his expression, but I could tell that it wasn't a happy one. He wasn't making sound anymore but his jaw was working, biting off his own tongue. Cassie came up the steps and sat down next to me. I kissed her neck and Kaylan deftly plucked out one of Walters's eyes and popped it into her mouth.

"Thanks," I said to Cassie, smiling. "You were right; I

do feel better."

"I'm glad," she said, resting her head against mine. "Come on, let's go. We'll clean up later."

Chloe was with Bradley in the living room, watching the first of what would be many Bogart movies. "We have something for you," Bradley told me, gesturing to the corner of the room. Leaning black and slender against the wall was the laser sight rifle. I picked it up, impressed by how light it was. I thanked Bradley and sat down awkwardly. Cassie plopped down next to me, asking Bradley what he'd managed to get out of Walters as Laura joined us on the couch.

"Well, he couldn't be relied upon one hundred per cent, of course," Bradley said, "but when he saw the basement I think he began telling the truth. Walters and his friends were rogues like us and not, as I'd first feared, part of a larger group. No one should come looking for them. We're quite safe."

This news went down well with all of us. I popped another pill and watched the movie, something complicated about murders and a detective. Before very long Cassie went back to the basement to help Mina and Kyle clean up. Laura put her arms around me and bit my shoulder softly. "I'm sorry," she said. "If we hadn't gone to that place on Quigley Street none of this would have happened."

"It's over now," I said, the downers washing me into a smooth sea. "It's one of those things. What's the word I'm looking for, Bradley?"

"Predestination, although you'd prefer the word karma."

"That's right," I nodded. "Karma, I like that. And I've got a new rifle, haven't I? That's something. What else did you swipe?"

"Plenty of fuel," said Chloe, "and lots of guns."

"There were some skin magazines in there too," said Bradley, "but we didn't have enough room for them. Sorry."

"So how did you find me?" I asked, surprised that I hadn't thought of this until now.

"Easy," Bradley said. "The truck would obviously stick to the widest roads, because of its size, and it was probably heading out of the City. I didn't think that Walters and his merry men lived around here because we'd have run into them before now. As cities go, this one isn't so big, and the sound of gunfire carries a long way. It also helped that they didn't see us as a threat, or they would have driven further and more quickly. After all, what did they actually see? Three kids running into a shop; hardly threatening behaviour."

"We were so worried," said Laura. "You should have seen Cassie, she went bananas. I thought she was going to shoot Bradley for letting you get caught, she had her gun to his head, but he stopped her by saying that he was the only one who knew how to get you back, and that she could kill him if we didn't find you. When we did find the truck Kyle had to hold her down to stop her charging right in there and getting killed."

"Surprise was essential," said Bradley. "We could only see one side of the truck so we didn't know whether there were more guards around. I worked my way to the side and Kyle stayed at the back. We shot the guards, there were only two of them, and the girls stormed the truck."

I tried to absorb all this but it wasn't easy getting my head around it. The only bit that really stood out was Cassie going bananas, which made me want to laugh. I kissed Laura's hair and Kyle appeared in the doorway, covered in blood. "I need a fucking wash," he said, and left. He was replaced by Cassie. She was holding two heavy looking black bags. In one of them something was moving sluggishly.

"Is that Walters?" asked Chloe, grimacing.

"Most of him," said Cassie happily. "His head and what's left of his chest started glowing a few minutes ago. His legs are still in the basement. You should decide what to do with him, Alex. Do you want to leave him as a zed?"

"No," I said. "We'll burn him."

Our first zed summer was over. We built the fire in the back garden and I impaled Walters's head on a stake in the middle of it. Cassie and Mina threw the rest of his body on and Bradley kindled a flame. Soon it was burning fiercely and as dusk fell Walters's hair caught fire and his jaw dropped open like he was screaming again, or laughing at us, I couldn't tell which. Cassie drank some bourbon and passed the bottle around. We all took a swallow, even Bradley, though it made him shudder and cough. When the bottle came back to Cassie she put it on the grass and held out her hands. We joined in a ring around the flames, Cassie holding my right hand, Laura my left.

"It isn't over for us yet," Cassie said. "We're growing stronger, closer, better. We're going to make it. Say something, Bradley."

I looked at Bradley over the flames, the shadows flickering across his face. He frowned, thinking, before closing his eyes and reciting in his piping voice;

"My formula for greatness in a human being is *amor fati*; that one wants nothing to be other than it is, not in the future, not in the past, not in all eternity. Not merely to endure that which happens of necessity, still less to dissemble it – but to *love* it."

We all dropped our hands, thinking about Bradley's typically weird quotation, smelling Walters burn and listening to the fat spit and crackle. My ass was sore as hell and my head was starting to spin. I went back into the house and smoked a cigarette in the living room, idly looking through the hundreds of CDs for some music I could listen to. Chloe walked in, smiling distantly. "I'm glad you're all right," she told me, and kissed my cheek. I puffed on my cigarette, not knowing what to say, and she left the room.

After failing to find any music I caught myself in the old habit of checking to see what was on TV. I laughed to myself and put the remote down. There was a glass bowl full of pretty looking downers standing on the coffee table. I crushed my cigarette and swallowed three more pills on the way to the bedroom. I watched the fire through the window until I couldn't stand up anymore then I undressed and collapsed on the bed, the cool sheets giving me shivers. The pills made it difficult for me to remember what had happened with the truck, or the faces of the men inside it. Pleased by this, I rolled under the sheets and watched the stars come out.

When I opened my eyes in the shadowy darkness I saw Cassie sitting on the edge of the bed. She was motionless, a statue. I tried telling her that her hair looked beautiful in the starlight but it just came out as a series of moans. My eyes were forcing themselves closed again. I fought it for I don't know how long before a cold hand touched my arm. Cassie was telling me something but I was too far gone and her words sounded like an exotic foreign language, incomprehensible.

Chapter 6

Our street had a solitary zed walking down it, a twentysomething man in a ruined suit. We walked towards him and I put the zed down. Cassie, Kyle and Mina were at my side. This was the first time I'd been out since the rape and I was surprised by how jittery I felt. Cassie had warned me about this but I hadn't really believed her. The house we were looking at, number ninety-nine, was imposing and decayed. The front gate had been left open and a car had been driven too fast up the driveway and had crashed into the garage door. The downstairs windows had been smashed and most of the tiles had fallen from the roof, exploded on the gravel below.

We were armed only with pistols. I'd wanted to bring the new rifle but it wouldn't be effective in confined quarters so I'd left it to be cleaned by Bradley in the armoury. A shower suddenly burst on us from nowhere so we hurried around the back and entered through the open door. There was old blood everywhere. A trail of it over the floor, dried pools on the dining room carpet, splashes on the silk wallpaper. A rotted meal was still set on the table and a bottle of wine had been knocked onto the floor. We moved through the hallway into the living room where a legless zed, a crawler, was dragging itself across the carpet like a clumsy snake. Mina shot it through the head.

Dusty family photographs lined the wall on the way upstairs. None of us looked at them. A little zed was sitting on the landing in its pyjamas. It made strangled sounds through its ripped up throat until Cassie put it down. She led us through the other rooms. We found a zed in the bath of all places, which helped lighten the mood. Another was flat out in its bed, probably a teenage girl, it was difficult to tell with its face gone. As I shot it Mina and Kyle began looking through the CDs in the rack, checking to see if there was anything they liked.

The last bedroom was made impressive by the enormous four-poster bed that stood in the middle of the floor. Cassie put down her gun and parted the yellowing nets. She climbed inside and called me over. I found her lying on silk sheets with her skirt pulled up. "I've always wanted to fuck on one of these," she explained, licking her fingers and pulling her underwear aside. "Come on, giddy up, what are you waiting for? A photo?"

The rain was heavier when we left and we'd have got soaked if Kyle hadn't noticed the umbrella stand that was hiding under the stairs. We splashed home through the puddles, Cassie with her arm around my waist under one umbrella, Mina and Kyle beneath another. Mina was swinging a bag that had inside it four CDs, a bottle of perfume, some lipstick that Mina thought Laura would like, two bottles of nail polish, moisturiser, hair-bands, a lighter and a little brass elephant.

The rain had slackened off by the evening and it was growing cold. Bradley had moved the rocket launcher into the lab to keep it dry. Now he was putting the finishing touches to Cassie's basement movie, which by now I dreaded seeing. I felt better after going outside though, it had been the right thing to do. Tonight was one of our whizz free nights so we drank gin and tonics instead. Laura, who had attended a few dancing lessons before the zeds came, was trying to teach Cassie how to tango. The haunting music Laura had put on made me yearn for something, but I didn't know what.

Chloe was sitting on the couch next to me. Her hair was getting long and she looked depressed, which wasn't surprising. When the whizz wasn't around to keep your spirits up everything could come crashing in. Sometimes it didn't matter but other times it could drive you out of your mind. The gin and the music weren't helping much either. I watched Laura lead Cassie around the floor, both of them with bare feet, concentrating hard. I finished my drink then poured more gin into my glass, not bothering to go to the fridge for the ice and the tonic. There weren't any lemons left anymore.

"How are things going with Kyle?" I asked Chloe inanely, but she didn't seem to hear me. She drank more gin and started to cry. I moved to put an arm around her but Chloe pushed me away.

"I'm fine," she said. "It's just the music. My father used to play it sometimes." Chloe began sobbing and staggered out of the room, glass in hand. I tried to empathise with Chloe's feelings but I was just too drunk so I watched the girls dance instead. It wasn't long before Mina breezed in. She looked at Cassie and Laura, crossing her arms.

"What are they doing?" Mina asked.

"The tango," I said.

"What for?"

"I don't know."

"Shut up," said Cassie. "This is hard."

"Quiet," ordered Laura. "Concentrate."

"This is stupid," said Mina. "What's the point of the tango anymore? Everybody's a zed now. Zeds don't dance."

"Shut up," repeated Cassie.

Mina made a face and poked her tongue out. I drank more gin and felt sick. My glass still had plenty left in it, which was bad. "I don't need to tango to have a good time," Mina said, taking my hand and dragging me upright. She marched me into her room, oblivious to my protests. Mina undressed quickly and struck a pose on the bed while I finished the gin. I put the glass down, took my clothes off, got into bed and passed out with Mina's insults ringing in my ears.

Cassie's basement movie was premiered the following afternoon. All seven of us had sat down to watch it. Cassie was very excited, rushing about and firing questions at Bradley about the finer points of editing. At last Cassie calmed down enough to put the tape on. I thought that the zeds didn't look as eerie on film as they did in the flesh, they were more like an elaborate special effect. Bradley had done a good job again and Mina's camerawork wasn't at all bad, although this wasn't a plus. To Cassie's consternation I walked out after five minutes, followed by Laura and Kyle. Chloe stayed, not having seen what we did in the basement before. As I left the room I saw Bradley smiling brightly from the chair in the corner.

The three of us went out into the garden where the sun had broken through and it was warm despite the breeze. We kicked a ball about for a while but I was still a little hungover and could only make a half-hearted effort. Kyle was worrying about what Chloe would think after seeing the movie. Laura pulled a sarcastic face and Kyle walked back into the house with his head bowed, talking to himself.

"I don't know why I put up with him for so long," Laura said. She kicked the football against the wall. It bounced off with a satisfying thwack. "You don't look so good," Laura told me.

"Hangover, and the movie." I fetched the ball and kicked it hard but I sliced it and it sailed over the wall. We heard it bounce on the road outside. "Shit," I said.

Laura laughed and sat on one of the deckchairs that Bradley had brought back out when the rain stopped. "I don't like seeing myself on film, either," Laura said. "It's creepy."

I agreed and sank into the other deckchair, asking Laura how the dancing had gone with Cassie.

"Pretty good," said Laura, "she learns fast. Do you remember me telling you about Mr Eliot, the first zed I saw? That's who I had lessons from. I gave it up after a few weeks though. He always had a hard-on, it was gross."

A picture of Mr Eliot, the dancing zed with the constant hard-on, came to my mind and I laughed. Laura asked me about the first zed that I'd seen.

"My brother, Tim," I said, remembering, watching the trees. "He began feeling ill in the afternoon. We didn't know what was wrong with him and the hospitals were full so we had to leave him in bed. He was older than me, nearly twenty. I went to a party that night, a bad one. There weren't many people there. I was drunk and I argued with my girlfriend about buying whizz. She hated whizz, she said that it made everyone boring. She left early, I don't know what happened to her.

"When I got home the next morning Tim was a zed. I found him in the kitchen, ripping chunks out of my father. It was just lucky I was still whizzing. When Tim looked up and came for me I ran like hell, back to Mikie's house where the party had been. He was still up, smoking with Lewis. They didn't believe what I told them of course, I couldn't blame them for that, but when we went outside it was obvious that something was wrong. It was quiet, and nothing was moving. There were dead dogs in the street. Then we heard someone screaming, and someone else from inside a house, pleading, then they started screaming too. That's when the zeds started to appear. Here, there, suddenly there were hundreds of the fuckers. They killed Lewis there and then. Mikie lasted a few more hours. I met Cassie a couple of days later."

Laura lit a cigarette and we sat there quietly until Mina came out of the house. "The film's still going," she told us, doing some aerobics on the grass. "We've just seen Alex and Kyle doing Marian, you should see the look on Chloe's face."

"It's just what she expected," said Laura.

"I'm not so sure," laughed Mina. "Where's the football gone?"

"I kicked it over the wall by mistake."

"Let's go and fetch it then."

Reluctantly I followed Mina to the armoury where we collected a pistol each. I could hear Cassie's moans coming from the television in the living room. We left through the front door and opened the gate. I peeped through the gap out into the street. No zeds. We made our way outside cautiously, the solid gate clicking shut behind us. I was beginning to feel nervous and I wished we'd brought some bigger guns. I still hadn't used the laser sight rifle. Wordlessly we crossed the wild grass that divided the properties and crossed into the street that ran behind our house. Predictably this street looked very similar to all the others. Hemdale Gardens was like a hall of fucking mirrors.

The football was nowhere to be seen. "Must have rolled under a car," said Mina. "Take this," she handed me her pistol, "keep watch while I find it." The first car was slewed across the pavement. I watched the empty street as Mina had a look underneath. There was nothing there so we moved to the next car. I closed its open door and saw a zed moving into view from the trees behind us. I shot it in the head. Mina was lying flat, reaching under the car. After a few seconds the ball rolled out, streaked with oil. Mina picked herself up and took the ball from the road. She walked up to our wall, shouting, "Hey! Laura!"

"Have you found it?" Laura shouted back.

"Catch!" cried Mina, kicking the ball over. Three zeds had appeared but none of them were close enough to worry about. We ran to the front of the house and headed for the gate. I shot at and missed another zed as Mina took out the remote and opened the gate. I put the zed down before going inside.

Chloe and Kyle spent most of the night arguing while we hit the whizz. Bradley had gone out on one of his secret missions again. I wondered what else he did out there in the dark other than collect weapons. It was probably better not knowing. Laura and Cassie danced around the floor as I talked to Mina, dabbing some whizz occasionally, clearing our mouths with water. Cassie seemed to understand us not wanting to be in the movie business. She said that we were all suffering from shyness and that we needed to express ourselves more.

After the girls had finished dancing we played cards for an hour, Laura coming out the big winner. I lost over twenty thousand. Then it was time for more lines and Cassie put one of her soft porn movies on. It was predictably terrible and made us all laugh. I tried to learn how to tango with Laura but I was useless and gave up after a few minutes, red faced. Bradley came home at three with bags under his arms, telling us that we had work to do tomorrow and that he'd explain all in the afternoon. We didn't allow his comments to spoil our night.

Paper masks, blue overalls and rubber gloves were spread over the kitchen table at which Bradley was sitting, looking stern, wearing his Juggernaut T-shirt. There was no room for my toast so I ate standing up. Laura took some water from the fridge, Kyle was brewing coffee. I avoided Bradley's stare by standing at the window. The leaves on the trees were still green and it looked like summer outside but the bite in the air reminded you that it wasn't.

Whatever Bradley had planned, I knew it wasn't going to be much fun, and I was sure that the others felt the same.

"I've counted at least forty-one corpses on the street outside," said Bradley. "No one's going to clean them up for us so we're going to have to do it ourselves. There's nothing to be gained in looking at me like that, we don't have a choice. Putrefaction breeds disease, don't you understand? We can't just leave them lying there."

The job took the rest of the afternoon. We piled the bodies onto a wagon that Bradley had brought home, Laura and Chloe keeping the zeds away, creating more bodies for us to shift. I only threw up once, when I dropped a corpse that burst open when it hit the ground. The lifting was heavy work but the whizz we'd taken made us strong. Each time the wagon was full we hauled it to the huge front driveway of number fifty-three. Within a few hours we'd created a bonfire of bodies. The disgust I felt at the work didn't fade or become easier to deal with as time went on. It was a horrible constant, bubbling away in my stomach and at the back of my throat. The smell was a revelation too, a multitude of stenches that all too easily penetrated our masks, our clothes, our hair.

When it finally came to an end I backed away with the others as Bradley poured petrol onto the pile and started the blaze. The bodies went up easily but none of us waited to watch the fire. We left the wagon where it was and trudged home, keeping our distance from each other, our masks discarded with the gloves and the overalls, eager to wash the stink from ourselves and to forget what we'd been doing.

As always, the downers did the trick. We watched some sci-fi movies that all looked the same, giggling at nothing, the room around us sliding out of focus. Past and future were abstractions, the zeds a vague possibility that couldn't bring us any harm. Chloe and Kyle were happy again, smiling into each other's eyes. I was lying on the carpet with Laura, melting into the floor. Cassie and Mina were kissing slowly on the couch. Bradley tried to lecture us about something but we couldn't help laughing at him so he walked away, scowling.

The cold woke me up at ten past four. I was still lying on the floor with Laura, but now we were naked, alone in the room. Someone had turned the lights out when they left. I hugged Laura but she was as cold as I was so I woke her up and we crept into her room and slid into bed, both of us shivering and dazed, icy hands interlocked.

"What the fuck are we going to do when winter comes?" I hissed to Laura under the sheets.

"Bradley will think of something," Laura whispered. "Get your bloody hand off! It's freezing!"

"Sorry," I said, putting my hand back into Laura's.

The laser sight rifle was great fun; just follow the red dot and, pop! I shot a zed in the mouth and it fell, looking surprised. I was standing with Chloe in a car park, the others were running around inside the supermarket. It was grey and blustery, rain drifting through the air like a shadow. I dropped four more zeds then stopped, puzzled. I turned to Chloe and saw that she was in the same situation. There weren't any zeds left standing. When we went food shopping the zeds never stopped coming, even if it was only one or two. They had this thing about supermarkets.

"What's going on?" Chloe asked me. I could only shrug. We waited, hearing shots from the supermarket then Cassie shouting something. Nothing unusual there. "This is too weird," muttered Chloe as we scanned the area. There was still nothing, just the small car park littered with about twenty bodies, a few forlorn looking cars and the silent rows of terraced houses that rose blankly around us. I coughed to give myself something to do. We could hear the zed wail in the damp air, so we knew they were out there, they just weren't coming for us. As Chloe had said, it was too weird.

It took another five minutes for the others to come out with their bulging trolley. The zeds had continued to stay away. Chloe explained things to Bradley as Kyle and Laura loaded up, using none of the frantic pace that was usually needed. I walked across the car park with Cassie and Mina, looking for the missing zeds. Just one would do. We stepped out onto the pavement and into the road, checking around the corner to the right.

"Nothing," said Cassie. "Come on, we'll go up here. Mina, keep that shotgun handy."

We crept up the road along the side of the supermarket until we reached the junction. The wails had been getting louder. We passed the supermarket and there on the left was a huge group of zeds, reaching for our faces and filling the road from side to side. We were back at the jeep in ten seconds, Chloe already revving the engine, alerted by our cries of terror. Bradley was waiting by the open door, wanting to know what was going on. "Get in the fucking jeep!" yelled Cassie, but Bradley's attention was diverted by the sight behind us. He looked surprised then did what Cassie had told him, the rest of us just behind. The zeds began converging in the car park and we left them to it.

"It could have been a freak occurrence," guessed Bradley on the way home.

"Maybe they're learning," I suggested.

"Anything's possible," nodded Bradley. "If they are learning we'll have to be more careful in the future."

"Fucking right," said Kyle. "The last thing we want is those cunts getting smart. What would have happened if they'd come around the corner when we were still inside? We'd be dogmeat."

"There is an alternative," said Bradley. "The zeds could have been waiting for us to leave. Perhaps they were deliberately avoiding confrontation, being less aggressive."

Cassie looked dubious. "Hippy zeds? I don't think so."

"Why not?" asked Bradley. "Aversion therapy. We'll wait and see what happens the next time, and the time after that."

"As long as we don't get killed," said Mina.

"We're going to live," stated Bradley adamantly.

The bottom of the wardrobe in our bedroom was choked with an array of shoes and boots. I hunted through them and finally found what I'd been looking for; Cassie's aluminium baseball bat. The gore had long been cleaned off it but it was still covered in dents. I took the bat out and turned to Cassie, who lay smoking in bed.

"You saved my life with this," I said, taking a few practice swings. "What's the story behind it?"

"My mother bought it in case my father ever came back." Cassie paused to drag on her cigarette. "She kept it in the corner of her bedroom."

"How many zeds did you kill with it?"

"I don't know. Count the dents. My arms were killing me by the time I found you in that church. What did you hide in there for, anyway?"

I shrugged. "It was free of zeds. Seemed like a good idea at the time, and if I hadn't hidden there we'd never have met."

"We were always going to meet," said Cassie, "all of us." She put her cigarette out and kissed the sleeping Laura on her nose. I took the bat and headed for the living room, where Kyle was fucking Mina on the couch. I left them to it and made my way to the library, which was frustratingly empty. I couldn't think of anything else to do so I went back to the bedroom to see Cassie, listening to Mina on the way.

Just as I was managing to fall asleep the door swung open. Mina poked her head inside. "Is anyone awake?" she stage whispered. "I don't want to sleep on my own." When we weren't drunk there wasn't enough room in the bed for four and Cassie hadn't moved so I got up and took Mina's hand.

"Thanks," she said, padding to her room. "It's so quiet tonight." We tumbled into bed and Mina switched off the lamp. I thought about all the zeds walking around on the other side of the wall. I wouldn't have wanted to sleep on my own either.

Over breakfast we decided what to do with the day. "We need warmer clothes," said Cassie, lining up her vitamins on the table. "We should hit the stores, check out the autumn sales. You wouldn't have to come, Alex."

"I'll be fine," I said, not knowing if this was true or not.

"We'll be more careful," said Kyle through a mouthful of toast. Cassie nodded. "So what does everyone think?"

We all agreed to the trip, Bradley being especially enthusiastic. He wanted to look at the pattern of the zeds' behaviour and pick up some books on sociology. We finished breakfast and I smoked a cigarette in the garden with Cassie. She was right about us need warmer clothes. I played on the swing, remembering the army truck and the sound of the crazy giggler, then I jumped off and chased Cassie around the garden to warm ourselves up.

The sun was setting by the time we arrived back home. The jeep was packed with coats, jackets, designer jeans and suits. The zeds behaved just as they always did; some aimless, others dangerous, a few deadly. I'd been too busy putting them down to worry much about army trucks. Bradley had taken me with him into the University bookshop, which was all the more spooky for its emptiness. I'd been relieved when we came back outside where at least the threat was visible. Cassie had led the expeditions into the clothes shops with Laura and Chloe. Mina stayed behind with the rest of us. I thought that Kyle must have done too much whizz, or maybe taken a few pills, because he'd started on some weird religious trip, preaching about eternal life to the heedless zeds and shrieking, "Praise Jesus!" every time he shot one. It was kind of disconcerting but I'd tried to ignore it and get on with the job, which hadn't been easy.

We held a party in the night, dressed in our new finery. Us boys wore tuxedos. Chloe had a long black dress, Cassie a sparkly red one, Mina a black suit, and Laura a blue. When the whizz was flowing we heaved the launcher back out onto the balcony and shot a few rockets into the sky, cheering at the explosions, hoping that they surprised some zeds. After that we held a race to see who could do the fastest ten inch line. Kyle won, but he forfeited his victory by succumbing to a sneezing fit. This meant that Chloe was declared the winner, with Cassie in second place, just ahead of me.

Before going to bed Bradley gave us a mercifully short lecture on decadence and corruption. For once we humoured him by listening but I don't think that anyone really knew where he was coming from. We were only interested in enjoying ourselves. I went down into the basement with Cassie and fucked Kaylan while Cassie worked on Marian. When we got back upstairs we found that Chloe and Kyle had disappeared into the garden, Laura telling us that they'd gone to look at the stars. We sank gin and tonics to get on an even keel and jabbered about who our favourite zed was. Mine was still Marian,

Cassie and Mina went for Lucy and Laura stuck with Kaylan. Cassie wanted to bring the camcorder out but we wouldn't let her so we compromised and took a few Polaroids instead. The best one showed the four of us jammed on the couch, trying to look happy but just looking manic and whizzy with glassy smiles stamped onto our faces.

Chapter 7

Our very first shopping expedition took place three days after we'd moved into the house. Bradley had already been exploring and had come up with a couple of rifles, which brought our total of guns up to four, though we didn't have any bullets left for the first one (Mina's pistol). We'd found out that Cassie was the best shot, followed by Bradley and Mina. This meant that I was the one stuck with the baseball bat. Leaving the security of our new house for the zed world outside seemed like madness or suicide, but food was running low, we didn't have any choice. We rode the streets for an hour, searching for the right kind of place. The zeds hadn't massed in the City Centre yet and their presence was everywhere. I was hungover and terrified but I wanted to impress Cassie so I did my best not to show it.

We finally stopped at a tiny supermarket that was jammed between a bakery and a seedy fast food place. I went inside with Bradley and ran through the aisles, quickly filling plastic bags with whatever food we could find. The place was dark and claustrophobic, zeds could have been fucking anywhere. We could hear a steady stream of shooting from outside. There didn't seem to be any zeds inside with us, though it didn't feel that way at all.

When the bags were full we ran back out onto the street and found Cassie and Mina standing back to back, the zeds surrounding us. Bradley shot a few as I jumped onto one bike and Cassie another. Bradley and Mina took the bags and swung themselves on behind us. We put our heads down and burst through the zeds, their icy hands clutching at us, ripping one of Bradley's bags away and nearly spilling us onto the road. It didn't take a genius to see that we couldn't do this for very long without getting killed. We didn't have enough people or enough firepower. There would have to be a change of plan.

That's when a big Mercedes came hurtling out of a side street and sped right at us. We barely got out of the way in time, falling to the road with the bags flying everywhere. The driver slammed on the brakes as the zeds moved in. We left the bikes and sprinted for the car, getting in and slamming the doors shut as a zed climbed onto the bonnet, slapping its hands on the windscreen.

The driver was a thin-faced girl in black jeans and a white T-shirt, older than the rest of us. She started to babble as the zeds began rocking the car. "Drive!" we all screamed. After a panicked second the girl understood and put the car into gear. She drove us over the zeds and into safety, telling us that her name was Chloe and that she'd been on the run for about two weeks, searching for survivors. She'd found two the week before but they'd been killed trying to refuel the car.

"Well," said Bradley, taking charge, "we've found a house over in Hemdale Gardens. It's very chic and there's plenty of room. Location, location, location. You're welcome to stay."

I was surprised to see that Chloe had doubts. "It's just the four of you? There aren't any others?"

Bradley was smiling sunnily. "If you mean whether our little group contains any adults that could be relied upon as authority figures then the answer, thankfully, is no. Size and age do not necessarily denote intelligence or adaptability. We are four children with an instinct to survive. We've made it this far and we aim to go on, and on."

Chloe seemed taken aback, which this time I understood. Because of the way Bradley liked to talk and the commanding presence he cultivated you expected him to have an immaculate side parting and a little tweed suit, not hair like a haystack and a Captain America T-shirt with baggy shorts that reached his scabby knees.

"I'm in," said Chloe finally. "Pleased to meet you."

"Likewise. I'm called Bradley. This is Cassandra, that's Mina and the bashful one back there is Alex."

Kyle was doing press-ups again, teeth gritted and red faced. He slowed down after twenty but managed to make forty three before collapsing and lying still. I was huddled on the couch with Cassie, wearing my new jeans and jacket, whizzing nicely but cold with it. Mina brought coffee in to warm us up, except for Kyle who looked warm enough already. He flexed his shoulders and put his shirt back on, saying something quietly to Laura. She shook her head and Kyle left the room looking unhappy. We drank our coffee and talked about what we'd wanted to do with our lives before the zeds had come along and fucked everything up. Disappointingly, no one had held any concrete ambitions.

"What about Bradley?" Mina asked.

"Good question," said Cassie. "Alex, go and ask him."

"Why me?"

"Because Bradley likes you the best," Cassie told me. "It's obvious. He makes fun of you more than he does the rest of us. It's his way of showing affection. Go on, ask him."

So off I went to Bradley's library, which was empty again. There was a light on in his room though, and the door was ajar. I knocked and it swung open. The stereo was on, playing some pop song with a twiddly guitar and a tacky keyboard solo. Bradley was running around the

110

room in time to the music, his hair slicked back, wearing a white shirt and a thin tie. It was difficult to tell whether he'd noticed me or not. Disturbed by this scene, I retreated to Kyle's room. He was lying naked on the bed, playing mournfully with his dick.

"What did you want to be when you got older?" I asked him.

"What a stupid fucking question," sighed Kyle. "Get over here."

I sucked Kyle's dick while he fingered me with blobs of KY. This would be the first time since the rape and I was feeling edgy but I forgot everything when Kyle started fucking me, rubbing more KY on my dick so it slipped through my hands. It wasn't long before we came, Kyle first, staying deep in my ass then pulling out slowly as I came over my stomach with shudders that made me cry out. I cleaned myself up then dressed, leaving Kyle to fall asleep. I needed a line and a cigarette, and a few drinks, but I stopped in the hallway before reaching the living room. The girls were playing a truth game. Intrigued, I decided to listen in.

"Are you ever glad that the zeds came?" asked Mina.

"Most of the time," said Cassie.

"Yes," said Chloe.

"Sometimes," said Laura.

"Do you fake it sometimes?" asked Chloe.

"Yes," said Mina.

"No," said Laura.

"Yes," said Cassie.

"Do you ever get turned on by killing zeds?" asked Laura, which I thought was a weird question.

"Of course not," said Chloe.

"No," said Cassie, "except for one time."

"No," said Mina.

"Have you ever fantasised about rape?" asked Cassie,

111

which was typical.

"No," said Mina.

"No," said Chloe.

"Yes," said Laura, "but only by zeds."

"Zeds can't get it up," pointed out Cassie.

"I know," said Laura, "but it's a fantasy. Anything can happen."

"What are you doing?" asked Bradley from behind me.

"Nothing," I said, striding into the room in a pathetic attempt at nonchalance. The girls exchanged glances. Bradley had messed his hair up and changed into his Doctor Doom T-shirt.

"You took your time," said Cassie, turning from me to Bradley. "Well?" she asked him.

Bradley blinked. "Well what?"

"Well, what's your answer?"

"Answer?"

"Right."

"Has Chloe taken to adding crack to your speed?"

"You what?"

"Or is it PCP?"

"What did you want to be when you grew up?" I said, ending this farce.

"Oh," said Bradley, nodding. "I'd always thought of becoming a hair dresser, but my genuine ambition, my true will, was to be a Mr Man. In fact, it still is."

"You're weird, Bradley," said Mina, but he ignored her and put another Bogart film on the video, taking his customary place in front of the television. I took care of my line, drinks, and cigarette, then I joined Bradley on the floor. The girls were talking about plans for tomorrow. I wanted to know what Bradley had been up to in his bedroom.

"What's that thing when you run around in a tie?" I

asked him.

"It's ceremonial," he told me, watching the screen. "I took the idea from a film of a concert. It reminds me that the business we're in is a serious one."

"How?"

"Because the ceremony itself is so absurd. It brings everything into perspective, stopping me seeing my existence in purely farcical terms, which would be all too easy, and deadly. Do you understand?"

"I think so. It's therapy again."

"Not exactly. Bogart up there is therapy. He makes a contribution to my sense of well-being. The ceremony doesn't do that."

"Sounds like it does."

"Then you don't understand," Bradley said, looking depressed.

"Watch this," said Kyle. The zed came closer and closer, dragging one broken leg behind it. Kyle was waiting with the shotgun socked into his shoulder. Only when the zed's face met the barrel did he pull the trigger, bursting the zed's head open like a party popper and spattering himself in gore. We all laughed as Kyle spat and wiped his eyes. There were thirteen bodies around us, most of them with their heads sliced off. Bradley had sharpened the swords this morning and their edges were keener than ever. It was another overcast day but at least it was dry. We'd ridden the bikes out of the City and onto the motorway, stopping here, at the first service station we'd come across. The car park we stood in was mostly empty. After sheathing the swords Laura lit a cigarette and we made our way to the services in front of us where more zeds would be waiting.

Four of them were watching us from just beyond the doorway. We put them down before stepping inside. The place was gloomier than expected and it took a while for our eyes to adjust. To our right was a fast food bar, on the left a wall of glass behind which was a shadowy restaurant. The arcade machines and shops were straight ahead. Laura blew some smoke rings before flicking her cigarette onto the floor. "Where to?" she asked.

"Forward," said Cassie. We began to move carefully, taking our time. We passed the fast food bar and a line of rotted plants. A zed thumped on the glass inside the restaurant but no one shot it. Dried blood had started appearing on the floor, not much at first but spreading quickly until it reached from wall to wall. Zed sounds grew audible, shuffles and moans. When we passed the restaurant they came for us, three from the black hole of the arcade, two from somewhere behind, six from the front. None of them got close.

We found most of the zeds congregated around the shop, some trying to get in, others on their way out. The majority didn't even seem to know we were there. Cassie and Mina were carrying the machine guns. They sent a deafening hail of bullets at the zeds who fell like bowling pins as the shop was decimated, the windows gone, tills exploding, magazines shredded before fluttering gently to the ground. It was an impressive scene.

We were all disappointed when the magazines were empty. The shop was unrecognisable, looking like a bomb had gone off inside. Zeds lay everywhere, many of them still moving feebly. Cassie and Mina reloaded while I stepped inside with Laura, over the broken glass, to see if we could pick up any cigarettes. Laura killed the injured zeds as I grabbed a few of the packs that hadn't been shot. There weren't very many. We rejoined the others under the cloud of gunsmoke that had risen to the ceiling.

"Let's go out the back," Mina suggested, "maybe they've got a park."

On the way out we passed the toilets and a line of slot machines. A zed was sitting on the floor. It had no arms and only half a leg. I shot it as we walked past and the zed almost looked grateful. When we got outside we saw that Mina had guessed right. Amongst the wild grass there stood a giant plastic snail, a little house, a roundabout, a see-saw, a slide that had been pushed over and some rusty swings. Seven or eight little zeds had been wandering about lethargically. Now they were heading our way. Cassie and Kyle took them down. The rest of us looked away.

We dragged the bodies inside and played around, having more fun than I thought we would. I hadn't been on a see-saw for years. Laura was with me, the others hurtled around the roundabout until Kyle fell off and banged his elbow. I smoked a cigarette inside the snail with Mina, reading the graffiti on the bright yellow shell. Cassie had climbed on top and was pretending to ride it. We could hear her bouncing up and down and shouting.

It didn't take long for the snail to fill with choking cigarette smoke so we crawled back out into the light. Cassie jumped down and gave us both a kiss, laughing at the smoke that was drifting out of the hole in the snail's side. The five of us grouped together and made our way back through the service station. A bunch of zeds had collected themselves outside the restaurant. The windows shattered beautifully as we put them down. A lot more zeds could be seen moving amidst the tables and along the counter. Kyle wanted to go inside and kill them but the rest of us had had enough for one day. We started walking back to our bikes with Kyle trailing grumpily behind.

"That was fun," said Cassie. "I liked that snail. We should get one, put it in the garden."

"I'd like a swimming pool," said Mina. I shot a zed that appeared from behind a truck. The fucker staggered but didn't fall. "I thought you couldn't miss with that thing," Mina told me, poking the rifle. I tried again and the zed hit the floor.

"Bloody hell," said Laura. "I've snapped a nail. Look."

Cassie peered at Laura's hand. "They were getting too long anyway. See the scratchmarks on my legs? You must have been a cat in a previous life."

"What kind of cat?" I asked.

"I don't know," said Cassie. "A tabby." She tickled Laura under her chin and meowed.

Bradley was full of questions, cornering me in the kitchen not long after we'd come home. I drank my coffee and did my best to humour him. "How would you describe the zeds' behaviour?" he asked, sitting opposite me at the table. "Were they less, or more aggressive than you've noticed in the past?" Bradley gave me a look that demanded an answer.

"They were just zeds," I said, thinking of the others who were safe in the living room.

"How did they react when you began to shoot?"

"They fell down dead."

"Please stop being obtuse. When the shooting began did the zeds make attempts to get out of the way?"

"I don't remember."

"Of course you remember! Think!"

"What does it matter?"

"It matters a great deal."

"Some of them just stood there," I said, finishing my coffee, "and some of them came for us."

"None of them turned away? Or even flinched?"

Laura and Cassie appeared hand in hand in the hallway, on their way to the bedroom. Laura laughed and blew me a kiss. Cassie beckoned with a finger before

116

Laura dragged her out of sight.

"I have to go," I told Bradley, "we'll do this another time."

"No! You'll just take some pills and then you genuinely won't be able to remember. We have to do this *now*. I don't understand your reluctance about this."

"None of the zeds turned away," I said, picturing the scene in the bedroom, the scene that was going on right now.

"Are you sure?"

"What? Yes, yes, can I go now?"

"What about the zeds in the park you told me about? The children. There weren't any adult zeds around?"

"Not that I saw."

"And while some adult zeds ignored you, none of the children did?"

"That's right."

"When you shot that zed and failed to kill it – Where are you going? This is important! You don't understand!"

The huge couch was like a welcoming cradle. I lay on it entwined with Mina, wanting to kiss her but paralysed by downers. Chloe and Kyle were watching a horror movie about a town that had slipped into another dimension. I thought that maybe that's what had happened to us. It made more sense than the zeds did. I tried to watch more of the movie but I couldn't get a connection. Mina's skin smelt of cocoa butter. She was saying something; "Nothing changes for us. We go out, we stay in. Zeds, guns, sex, whizz, pills. It's, it's just-"

"Just what?"

"It's like we're running in circles, repeating ourselves, and that's the way it's always going to be."

This didn't make any sense to me but what did it matter? We were alive, we were in love. Life was fun. I

117

yawned, my body growing numb. Someone screamed on TV and Chloe scowled. Kyle laughed. My eyes were closing but I grimly hung onto consciousness. I didn't want the day to end yet. It had gone so well, apart from Bradley's interrogation. Why couldn't he just relax? He was so stressed all the time, with his questions and his books and his weird ceremonies. Even his jokes were a serious business, even his *therapy* was. He needed to kick back, go with the flow. After all, stress was a killer, everybody knew that. Then I noticed that Bradley had appeared in the room, there he was on the floor.

"Bradley," I called, "hey, Bradley." I finally managed to get his attention. It was time to tell *him* something for a change, and I did. "Take a back seat," I said. "There's no need to be so worked up all the time. Ease down, you know? Enjoy yourself, have some fun. Be happy now and then, it won't kill you. What do you think?"

Bradley looked at me blankly for a few seconds, no doubt considering my advice. "Look at you!" he suddenly exploded, making me jump. "Look at the state you're in! You can't even talk! Do you realise this? You sound like you're six months old, all gurgles and grunts. What could you possibly be trying to tell me? That your nappy needs changing? No! I know! You've worked out what we should do if one of us gets accidentally shot, or fractures a bone, or needs their appendix removed. You've solved the problem of long term food shortage! No? Then you've discovered a fresh water spring at the bottom of the garden amongst the fairies, hooray!

"It's none of these things? Then what could it be? Of course! You're telling me that you'll know what to do when one of the girls gets pregnant, it's so obvious. Well done, Alex, I always knew I could count on you. Now I won't have to think of anything by myself anymore. Instead I'll blow my brains out with narcotics, live for

118

cheap sex, take great pleasure in torturing largely mindless creatures and to round it all off I think I'll video myself gang raping some walking corpses down in the basement! What could be better?"

With that Bradley left the room, closing the door gently behind him. I was as amazed as all the downers inside me would allow. Bradley kept his cool at all times, he *never* lost it. What had I done? I noticed that everyone in the room was looking at me.

"Nice going, Alex," said Chloe, lighting up a cigarette.

"I just wanted to help," I said miserably.

"Don't worry," consoled Mina. "Bradley was just letting off steam. He didn't mean the things he said."

We all heard him leaving the armoury and going out through the front door. I wondered if he was thinking of coming back. Suddenly, passing out seemed like a very good idea. I heaved myself off the couch and headed for Mina's room, for once wanting to be alone. I rolled into bed and dropped like a stone into darkness.

Early the next morning I was alone in the kitchen, making myself breakfast. My mind felt muddy and slow. I was looking forward to some whizz in the afternoon to sharpen me up. The kettle was just boiling when I heard a door open and someone moving through the hallway. I fervently hoped that it wouldn't be Bradley but, of course, it was. His hair was messier than ever and he looked very tired. He was wearing his Incredible Hulk T-shirt.

"It was weak and impolite of me to blow up like that," he told me. "I'm sorry. It won't happen again." Bradley turned to go but Cassie had appeared behind him, blocking the doorway. By the expression on her face I guessed that Mina had told her what had happened. She marched Bradley through to the living room. As soon as the door closed she began shouting at him. My toast was about to burn. I popped it up and closed the kitchen door to block out Cassie's voice. By the time I'd eaten and smoked a cigarette Bradley was back in his library and Cassie was in the kitchen with me, her face still dark.

"I hope you weren't too hard on Bradley," I said, feeling sorry for him.

"Fuck that weirdo," snapped Cassie. "He should be more careful where he takes out his frustrations. He won't be doing it again, though. Jesus, he's repressed."

"What did you say to him?"

"That doesn't matter. What are you looking so mournful for? I look around this house and all I see are unhappy faces. You all need cheering up. I'll start right now with you. Just watch what I do with this … What do you know, you look better already, what a surprise."

I'd been convinced that the chances of me riding into the City at night were one in a million, and that the chances of me walking there were flat cold zero, but here I was, doing just that. Bradley had cornered me in the hallway at nine o'clock. I couldn't tell what T-shirt he'd been wearing because he'd put on a black jacket. His trousers were black too. I'd faced him warily, thinking that he was going to tell me something I didn't want to hear.

"Come with me," he'd said quietly. "I want to show you something. Wait, come back here. Listen. It's an adventure, and it's a lot safer than going out on those motorcycles in the middle of the day."

"Where are you going?" I'd asked reluctantly.

"Into the City," Bradley had answered.

"How are you going to get there?"

"On foot."

"And you expect me to tag along?"

"Only if you want to."

"I don't."

"You will."

"Why's that?"

"You'll see when we arrive. Don't be afraid. The zeds can't see well at night, they're not cats. I've been out at night many times, haven't I? I've never had to fire a shot. The risk is minimal, and it's well worth it. Trust me. You shouldn't let this opportunity slip by."

We'd argued for a few more minutes but Bradley won, as he always did. I changed into black clothes and put on the hat that Bradley offered. We'd painted our faces like commandos then Bradley brought some pistols from the armoury. They had silencers attached to them. I took one of the guns and two spare clips, listening to the music pump from the living room. We left the house and moved down the driveway. Bradley opened the gate and we crept into the zed night.

This was the first week of October and the air was calm but biting hard. The sky was cloudless and the moon thin. The stars shed enough light for us to see by. As far as I could tell we were the only moving things on the street. Cassie must have been wondering where I was. She'd assume I was down in the basement, which when I thought about it was exactly where I should have been. What the fuck was I thinking of? Going through with this was insane.

"I'm not sure about this anymore," I whispered. "We should turn back."

"Go ahead," said Bradley. "No one's holding a gun to your head."

We'd already passed into the next street. The thought of going back alone froze my heart, as Bradley well knew. I was stuck with the little maniac. This thought gave me a perverse hope, my misguided positivity undoubtedly down to the whizz I'd been taking all day. I tried to smile bravely to myself and I'd just succeeded when a single zed wail sounded from what felt like six inches from my left ear. I jumped and spun, pistol ready, only to find that the street was empty. I stood still, waiting for the next sound, wishing my hands were steady.

"Try and get used to it," Bradley said. "Everything sounds different at night, and please don't be so eager to shoot. A silenced pistol is anything but silent. The only way we'll be in danger is if we make too much noise."

"Then keep your voice down," I snapped in a whisper.

Bradley smiled and we carried on, leaving Hemdale Gardens after twenty minutes of desolate repetition, house after fine dead house, car after expensive empty car. There were more wails and other, inexplicable sounds, but we didn't spot any zeds until we reached Matheson Avenue, where the houses were older and built closer together. The zeds were moving in someone's front garden, one of them pressing itself against the house, the other just slouching around like it was looking for something to do. We crossed the street and walked past them, unseen.

The walk had warmed me up and I was beginning to sweat. I took off my hat and stuffed it in my back pocket. Another zed was standing in the street, a fat man in shorts with a mauled face. As we went by I fought the urge to put a bullet in its head. The zeds were a different proposition out here in the dark. That zed glow was really coming into its own, haunting and beautiful by turns, pressing home just who the City belonged to. The living had gone out of fashion.

As the journey went on the zeds inevitably grew more numerous. Some streets were too busy and had to be avoided, others seemed deserted but proved not to be. I didn't speak much with Bradley and, bar directions, he didn't say anything to me. We just did our best to keep out of the zeds' way, heading into the City, which I still couldn't believe I was doing. What the fuck did Bradley want to show me there? Zed happy families? Despite these doubts I thought I was handling things well. The two of us were miles from light and security, on foot, armed only with pop guns and surrounded by zeds who wanted to tear us apart. It seemed like I was better off when I'd been on the run with Cassie, but it didn't feel that way.

Commerce had moved in around us after a couple of hours of walking. We were flanked by tall buildings that used to house insurance companies and investment firms. It was darker here as the buildings crowded out what little light there was available. I thought I'd see more zeds in suits but I was proved wrong, in fact there weren't many zeds around at all. The most we saw were converged around the infirmary car park. Two ambulances had crashed into a police car. A security fence had been torn down from the main doors.

"I think you might like it here," whispered Bradley. "Lots of pretty zeds wearing nurses' uniforms."

"Fuck you," I said, poking Bradley with my pistol, keeping an eye out for the zeds that he'd mentioned.

Our humour died down as we got closer to our goal. The zed wail was growing louder all the time and we were headed right for it. I decided that I'd seen enough already to make the trip interesting, I'd had adventure enough for one night. What was the point of carrying on? We'd reached this far without trouble, it would be stupid to push our luck any more. I tried to work out more eloquent arguments than these to persuade Bradley to turn back. After some hard thinking I came up with nothing. Speaking wasn't easy, anyway; my throat was too dry.

We were only minutes away from the centre now and things were getting crowded. I counted over fifty zeds scattered in front of us, all of them heading the same way we were. What was shredding my nerves even more than this sight was the wail, making me shiver as I walked, louder with each step. I had to keep checking to see if Bradley was still leading the way on my left. He was striding confidently, head moving all the time, his gun hidden in his jacket. He turned suddenly into another street where I could only see four zeds. We slipped by without trouble and carried on.

The first shops began to appear in dingy alleyways, all of them with their windows shattered, sports shoes, clothes and CDs trampled underfoot by the zeds. We skirted these places and headed through more streets, heading away from the centre now. Just as I was feeling relieved Bradley took two more turns and we started heading back. I was about to complain when I noticed that the zeds had disappeared. This area was much like others we'd been passing through recently, the offices gone, replaced by worn terraced houses with no gardens, most of them with their doors hanging open.

"Where have the zeds gone?" I whispered. "What's happening?"

Bradley glanced at me. "Be patient, you'll soon see."

"No!" I was in no mood for patience. "Tell me now!"

"There aren't any zeds here because this road doesn't give direct access to the City Centre."

This sounded like good news to me. I did my best to shut off the spiralling zed wail as the street came to an end with a supermarket on the right and a mechanic's on the left. In front of us was a lowered barrier that guarded a car park. After the car park stood a series of tall, wide buildings that hulked across in both directions. Something was moving in the supermarket, a zed. Maybe more than one. The glow was casting shadows on the wall.

"We've arrived," said Bradley. He ducked under the barrier and trotted past the three cars that were parked here. I was close behind. The building we approached had two entrances, one for cars, very wide and covered by a steel grille, the other for people, a sturdy looking door. As we reached it Bradley took a set of keys from his pocket. He chose one from the ring and unlocked the door, which opened without a sound.

We stepped into a black corridor and Bradley passed me a torch. He unlocked the roof access door then closed the one we'd come through, plunging us into perfect darkness. I gasped in horror before remembering the torch, flicking it on and seeing a flight of stairs rising before me. Bradley led me through then locked the door behind us.

"We're safe now," he said aloud. "I always keep this door locked." He took the torch and started up the stairs, twisting left then right. The wail was largely muffled here. We climbed for three floors before reaching *another* fucking door. My legs ached and my breath puffed in clouds around me.

"This is it," said Bradley. "I found this place some months ago. I took the keys from the supervisor's office and locked the building, which was filled with zeds. I shot them all and threw them down into the basement. I found it hard work, but it was worth it. Are you ready?"

Without waiting for an answer Bradley opened the door and walked through. We stood on a wide, flat rooftop surrounded by a concrete lip. The zed wail was enormous, a tremendous sexless voice that brushed my senses away and shook me until my teeth rattled. The light was brighter here too, much brighter. Bradley was standing at the edge of the roof with his hat in his hand. I joined him, forgetting who I was when I saw what was waiting there, thirty metres down in Zed City Centre. The ground was heaving with thousands upon thousands of shining zeds packed shoulder to shoulder on their way to nowhere, a seething zed river. It flowed without thought or feeling, the collection of light burning my eyes.

"It's a powerful sight," shouted Bradley over the wail. "It demonstrates how the zeds beat us. Their purpose is singular. Now that they've won, what will they do?

Every city on earth must look like this, and for what?" Bradley frowned as he watched the scene unfolding below. "What time is it?" he asked.

I checked my watch. "Twelve thirty."

"We'll stay until one," said Bradley. "Keep looking."

Chapter 8

It had been Cassie's idea to take a bed from one of the spare rooms and move it into ours. "Now we won't have to worry about who sleeps with who," she'd explained, "and if anyone wants to be on their own, there's always Laura's room, or Mina's." The job took much of the day. It didn't help when Kyle refused to do any work, saying that it was nothing to do with him. He spent the afternoon upstairs in the lab with our chemist.

First we had to move two wardrobes to the other side of our room, which wasn't at all easy. After that was done we rested and complained about the lack of whizz that was around when we really needed it. Next we had to shift a dresser in the spare bedroom, then another wardrobe, this one full of Laura's castoffs. We took a second, longer rest, then started on the bed. The mattress was simple enough but the bed itself was a different matter. After ten minutes of heaving we managed to get it stuck in the doorway. I was in the hall with Mina, pulling as hard as I could. It wasn't long before the bed crushed Mina's foot. Her hopping wails brought Bradley from his library.

"You morons," he said. "What do you think you're doing?"

"Shut up, Bradley," cried Cassie, invisible in the spare room. "Go away."

Bradley did just that, but he came back with a screwdriver in his hand. Under his instructions we pushed the bed back into the room where Bradley promptly unscrewed it into two parts, provoking red faces all round.

"What do you want two beds in one room for,

anyway?" he wanted to know. "There's something wrong with all of you." We bit our tongues and moved the bed into our room. Bradley screwed it back together again and left without another word. After putting sheets on the new bed we pushed the two of them together and surveyed our handiwork. There wasn't as much room to move in anymore but it looked fine.

"Well, what are we waiting for?" Cassie asked us. "Let's try it out."

Fucking in a quadruple sized bed was a lot of fun but you had to be careful not to fall down the gap in the middle. Not having taken any whizz I came quite (very) quickly and wasn't much use after that so I pulled some trousers on and smoked a few cigarettes in the living room. When it was time I made four drinks and took them on a tray to the bedroom. Laura was already asleep, a shapeless hump under the covers with blonde hair trailing up over the pillow. Cassie and Mina were lying spread-eagled, flushed and happy. I handed them their glasses and hopped onto the bed next to Mina.

"What shall we drink to?" I asked.

"To life without pain," answered Cassie.

"Life without pain," I echoed with Mina.

We touched glasses and drank, listening to Laura's sleep-heavy breathing. Tomorrow was going to be another shopping day. We were going to hit the same store as last time to check if the zeds would act as they'd done before. I didn't think they would. I hadn't been out since the journey into the City with Bradley last week. I'd tried explaining to the others what I'd seen but I hadn't found it easy and I didn't think they'd really understood. I wasn't sure that I'd really understood it either. I decided to concentrate on finishing my drink and to forget everything else. When I'd managed this I put my glass on the dresser and got under the sheets with Laura. I held her, enjoying her warmth, closing my eyes.

"Look at those two," said Cassie to Mina. "They'd sleep their lives away if they had the chance."

"Stop it," said Mina, "it tickles."

"Does this tickle?"

"Oh no, it doesn't tickle at all, not at all."

"How about this?"

Mina shrieked, making Laura grumble.

"Sorry," Cassie said, not sounding it at all.

The zeds stayed true to form during the shopping expedition. Instead of staying away they came for us in huge numbers, provoking a pitched battle in the car park. Without the machine guns we'd have been finished. Cassie killed three zeds with one shotgun blast, impressing everyone except Chloe, who hadn't been looking, and Bradley, who pretended not to notice.

It hadn't taken very long for us to see that we weren't going to get any shopping done today. The tide of determined zeds showed no sign of ebbing and our ammunition was beginning to run low. Laura was the first to stop shooting. The rest of us quickly joined her. As the zeds kept climbing over the hill of their former comrades we ducked into the jeep and Chloe drove us away, mood despondent.

Cassie and Kyle were fucking in the bedroom. Laura and Mina clutched each other on the couch, watching a horror movie about a pretty girl in her underwear who was trapped in an old hospital that was run by an insane doctor who just might be the girl's father. Bradley had left just as the film was starting, telling us that he had data to sift, fooling no one. I did more whizz and lit a cigarette, listening to the girl scream on the TV. Chloe the chemist was sitting next to me wearing a smart dark suit that made her look older than she was.

"This film's rubbish," Chloe said scathingly. "What are you two so frightened for?" Laura and Mina flinched in answer. "It's stupid," continued Chloe, "you see scarier things than this every time you go outside, but it doesn't bother you then. Why be brave about something that's real then be scared about something that's false?"

Mina shot Chloe an evil look then turned back to the screen. Chloe looked surprised, shrugged an apology and cut some lines out on the table. "I was only asking," she said.

After the film finished Mina put another one on, this time about a girl who had a dark secret. Laura and Mina didn't seem to find this movie so scary. I talked with Chloe about where we should go shopping tomorrow. She suggested Glover Street, wherever that was. I wondered how long it would take us before we'd hit every supermarket around the City. Chloe thought it would take some time.

We were listening to Frank when Cassie came in. She snorted two gigantic lines then poured herself some tequila and told Chloe that Kyle was in her bedroom, wanting to talk. Chloe left with a sigh and Cassie took her place next to me. I could hear Mina jabbering to Laura about aquariums. I asked Cassie what Kyle wanted to talk to Chloe about.

"He said that he wanted to talk about God," said Cassie, laughing. "Not all of God, just His Finger, or His Hand. Kyle thinks that God has Pointed at us, and especially at him. Kyle is the Chosen One."

"What's wrong with him?" I asked, worried.

"Megalomania," said Cassie. "It's the only way he can cope. Tell me what you saw outside with Bradley again."

I groaned. "I've told you plenty of times. You know everything I know."

130

Cassie sucked on her cigarette and narrowed her eyes. She blew smoke at me then changed the subject. "We played a truth game last week. It was interesting. I learnt a lot of things."

"Like what?" I asked, trying to sound genuine, failing.

"You know," said Cassie, "this and that."

I hurriedly cut more lines out. Two for me, two for Mina, two for Laura. After doing mine I called the girls over, hoping that this would distract Cassie. The music had finished and we could all hear Chloe and Kyle arguing, which I thought was kind of predictable. Mina was busy putting her hair back into a ponytail. "Chloe's been a bit of a bitch recently," she said.

The supermarket on Glover Street was small but well stocked, and it only had one entrance. I was inside with Bradley and Mina. The shelves surrounding us were only stacked waist high so it was easy to check for zeds. The only ones we had to watch out for were the crawlers. Some of them could drag themselves across the floor with scary speed. We stocked up on food first, Mina piling on packet after packet of noodles. When we were finished we darted outside and loaded the jeep. This was a fairly wide open area, a grass verge dividing the road, a row of tall houses opposite us. The zeds were well spread out and particularly slow, no problem for the others.

Cassie took Bradley's place and we went back inside for alcohol and cigarettes. We took a few cartons and as many bottles that we could carry. On the way out we passed Laura and Kyle, who were collecting the water. I helped put down some zeds as Cassie loaded up with Mina. By the time they'd finished Laura and Kyle were back. They put the water in the jeep and the job was done.

"I wish it could always go this smoothly," said Chloe as she opened the door.

Kyle disagreed. "Where would be the fun in that? It would be fucking boring."

I shot a tall thin zed before sliding in next to Laura. I mistakenly poked her in the leg with my rifle and she told me to be more careful. Chloe drove up past a theatre that I hadn't seen before. It was fronted by a glass construction with red piping. About ten zeds could be seen milling around inside, bumping into chairs and tables, oblivious to the broken glass that covered the floor.

"I went there last year with school to see a play," said Laura, looking back at the theatre as we drove by.

"Which play was it?" asked Bradley.

"I don't remember," said Laura, "but they had nice costumes."

We were all hungry when we got home so I helped Mina boil a huge saucepan full of noodles that the seven of us ate together in the living room. The food was pasty and tasteless but the wine made up for it. By the time Bradley had disappeared we were very drunk, dotted around the living room, listening to Frank yet again. I was getting tired of him. I sat dazed in an armchair with a newly opened bottle in my hand. Where were the cigarettes?

"Mina," I called, though she didn't smoke. "Cigarette?"

Mina weaved her way towards me as Cassie and Kyle shouted happily. Mina's mouth was smeared with wine stains, which meant that mine probably was as well. Mina magically pulled a cigarette from her pocket and laughed. I swapped it for my wine. Mina took a swallow as I lit up then she sat down heavily on my lap and gave me a sloppy kiss.

"I'm sick of Frank," I slurred. "We should listen to something else."

"Fuck off! Don't be so stupid. Frank's the best." Mina

poured wine down my throat and spilled some over my T-shirt. "Just, just listen to his voice. Do you hear it? Frank still speaks to us, you can't get sick of him, it's impossible, see?"

Mina punched me three times to hammer her point home. Cassie and Laura were trying to tango again but this time they were too drunk. Within seconds they'd tripped over each other's feet and were rolling on the carpet while Chloe applauded and laughed. Kyle came up with the idea of going into the garden so out we trooped into the clear night. Kyle began singing tunelessly and staggered off around the side of the house. It was cold outside but the alcohol was like an overcoat so it didn't bother any of us. I took the bottle back off Mina and gulped some wine down, looking at the whirling sky.

Cassie dropped to her knees and started to howl joyously at the moon. It didn't take long for Mina then Laura to join in, the girls kneeling in a triangle on the grass with their hands cupped to their mouths, calling the zeds for miles around. Chloe put her hands over her ears and said something before going back inside. I drank more wine and searched for Kyle. He wasn't far away, passed out on the garden path.

The girls had stopped howling and were finishing off another bottle. Cassie drank the last then hurled the bottle over the wall. It hit a car on the street and exploded with a satisfying sound. I explained what had happened to Kyle. The four of us had to carry him deadweight back into the house. He fought us as much as he could from his stupor and groaned thickly. We left him on the carpet in the dining room.

"What's next?" Cassie asked us in a hoarse voice.

Laura claimed the bottle from me. "The basement," she said.

"Of course!" cried Cassie, emulating Bradley.

We ran into the kitchen and opened the basement door. Cassie turned on the light and the four of us clattered down the steps, holding onto each other to stop ourselves falling. "Hel-lo!" trumpeted Cassie to our zeds. She rushed over to Lucy and jumped on her. Mina headed for Kaylan. I undressed with Laura and staggered over to the glaring Marian. We slackened her chains and pushed her onto the carpet. Laura giggled and took a gulp of wine, opening her mouth and letting the drink spill out over Marian's face. We licked it up with purple tongues, meeting over the zed's gag and kissing. I saw that Cassie was naked and had wrapped her underwear around Lucy's neck, trying to strangle her with it. Mina was entwined with Kaylan on the floor.

I choked Marian a little to calm her down and Laura pushed the zed's legs open. She poured wine over Marian's glowing cunt and put her mouth to it, waving me back as the zed's legs slid around her shoulders. I'd finished the wine before Laura pulled herself away. She squeezed my dick then I fucked Marian for a few giddy minutes, sucking on Laura's small tits. When my cock felt like nothing less than an icicle I moved away and got myself behind Laura. She hissed as I started to fuck her.

The change between Marian's cold and Laura's heat was bringing me to a drunken climax. Cassie appeared and positioned herself between Laura and Marian. Cassie talked to the zed, slapping her then greasing up her right hand. She began forcing it into Marian's cunt, her other hand wrapped around the zed's white throat. When Laura spread Cassie's ass and began licking it everything around me started breaking up. I was fucking Laura on automatic, my impending orgasm distant and unreal. An icy hand wrapped itself around my balls and Mina slid her tongue into my ear. Amidst the fuzzy colours I made out the surreal sight of Cassie's hand disappearing into the zed up to the wrist. As I came I turned to Mina and she kissed me, her tongue frozen over mine. I tumbled backwards onto the carpet and my vision fractured sickeningly. Three separate versions of Mina were putting their faces between six of Laura's legs.

"Do it," I heard Laura say as I closed my eyes and started to ride on the invisible rollercoaster. "Do it, do it, do it."

A crushing hangover woke me up a few hours later. At first I had no idea where I was but when I managed to open my eyes I saw with a groan that I was still down in the basement. There was Kaylan, looking right at me. So were the other two zeds. They had been chained back onto the wall and stood in the way that only zeds can; perfectly still, unbreathing. You'd have been sure they were statues if it hadn't been for their eyes, staring with flat zed intensity. Those eyes followed me as I crawled naked for the steps, shivering all the while. When I finally reached them I grabbed the banister and swung myself to my feet with nausea oozing from my pores. I forced myself up the steps without looking back and left the zeds alone.

Chloe hadn't been easy to live with for the first few days. She was impatient and irritable, getting drunk every night and throwing up before she passed out. I fucked her during this period, an intense and somehow solitary experience. Chloe ignored me for the next twenty-four hours. Understandably, we'd all thought that Chloe was acting this way due to her zed experiences. We all had horror stories to tell and it was hard for everyone trying to adjust to each other and to our new lives. We were wrong, though; Chloe just wanted whizz. As much as possible, as soon as possible.

After a week Chloe cracked and told Bradley what

was wrong. This led to a trip to the pharmacy that very day. We couldn't stay as long as Chloe would have liked, due to the array of zeds that had been moving in, but when we got home we were pleasantly surprised by the amount of pills that Chloe had managed to collect. She arranged them into different categories on the kitchen table, describing their effects in detail for us, popping the whizz pills like sweets. I'd headed straight for the morphine and the hypnotics, Cassie and Mina not far behind.

The next twenty-two days were a swampy haze where I lost six kilos and much of my mind. I forgot about the zeds and spent much of my time lying flat on the carpet and communicating telepathically with Cassie and Mina, which I found a lot easier than speaking. Laura and Kyle quickly agreed to join our happy band and came home with Chloe and Bradley.

It took me three whole days to notice our new recruits. Neither of them seemed able to communicate telepathically so conversation was impossible. What did it matter? Along with Cassie and Mina I was evolving into something that was more than human, an artist in all my ways. The waking world and the dreaming had intermingled, I was both man and butterfly. I couldn't possibly have hoped for anything more, at least until the pills ran out. Then we had to get more. Bradley refused to help. So did Chloe. Same with Kyle. Laura said nothing at all, she just stared. We knew that the three of us had no chance of hitting a pharmacy and getting out alive. Bradley told us that we needed focus to deal with the zeds, that the pills would get us all killed. I tried to hit him but I was too weak. We climbed the walls for six days, throwing up, unable to sleep, sweating and shivering together in the bed. When we finally came out of it we got drunk, vowing never to touch the hard stuff again and only to stick with the soft.

Even without the mind-bending pills I was finding it difficult getting anywhere with Laura. She refused to leave the house and stuck to Kyle's side as much as she could, nervous on the rare occasions when they were apart, clutching herself with her eyes fixed to the floor, lips trembling. Whizz was the only thing that could make her say more than one sentence at a time, and even then her voice never rose above a whisper. Kyle was very different, laughing loud and telling stories, seeing the zed situation as a huge adventure to be enjoyed. To me it felt like the seven of us together just wasn't going to work out.

It had taken us hours to find this cove but when we arrived it was worth it. Cliffs frowned on either side of the outgoing sea. The car park was a wide piece of waste ground behind us. At the base of the cliff a couple of hundred metres to the right a hotel was standing, half of it eaten by fire. There were still some cars parked outside it. A zed was wandering lazily towards us through the surf on the left. It wouldn't reach us for a while yet. A few more were moving in from the hotel.

We'd been kept inside the house for nearly a week, hiding from the weather. The garden became a swamp and the gutters had clogged. The sky looked like a boiling cauldron and the rain had transformed the street outside into a river. Our mood became predictably claustrophobic, arguments never more than one remark away. Whizz didn't help much and alcohol not at all. Downers did the trick, keeping many of the black thoughts submerged where they couldn't do much harm. Typically, Bradley had been in high spirits, whistling his way around the house, annoying everyone with his chirpiness and his casual remarks about how those with the least imagination always succumbed to cabin fever first. Eventually Cassie had thrown a cup of coffee at him, yelling, "Just fuck off!"

The rain had stopped late on Saturday night and the wind had died down the following morning. I spent Sunday afternoon on the roof with Bradley, clearing out the guttering, which was mostly filled with disgusting leafy mush. Bradley strolled around the roof wearing his Spiderman T-shirt, chatting amiably about the job his father used to do, something about building sites. He'd fallen down a hole and broken both his legs, then tried unsuccessfully to sue for damages after seeing an advert on TV. He'd ended up having to pay legal costs and tried to commit suicide by rolling in his wheelchair in front of an oncoming train, but someone grabbed the wheelchair in time and Bradley's father only fell onto the floor, fracturing his wrist when he hit the ground.

Laura took her boots off and went to paddle in the shadows. Kyle skimmed stones over the water, counting aloud the bounces they made before plopping into the sea. Eight was his best so far. Mina was perched on a rock with a rifle across her knees, watching the zeds get closer. Cassie was sitting on the sand with me. I was finding the salty air a strain on my lungs and I kept wanting to cough.

"Ten!" cried Kyle, fist in the air.

Cassie's birthday was getting closer, I didn't know how many days away but it was soon. I'd have to check the calendar when we got home. We needed to take a trip into the City to get presents. "Heads up," said Mina. The single zed on the left was coming into range. This one had been a middle-aged woman, all I could tell from this distance. She was wading through the sea with her arms held stiff at her sides. Mina stood up and sighted. After a short pause she pulled the trigger and the zed collapsed into the water. The body floated, spinning gracefully before being sucked out to sea.

"Fish food," Mina said. She settled back on her rock and closed her eyes peacefully.

138

"We should live closer to a place like this," said Cassie. "I really miss the sea."

It didn't look like Kyle was going to better his record of ten, not that he would see it that way. He kept throwing but his action had gone and he couldn't get more than six. Laura turned to the zeds that were coming from the hotel, waves washing over her ankles. The zeds would have to be put down soon. I took the rifle and walked towards them, stopping when I was close enough for an easy kill. I looked through the sight and there was a pretty young zed with black hair and a red spot shining on her forehead. Pop, and she fell. The next one was closer, a stringy man who'd been ripped up badly. Down he went. There were still three left, an old woman, a man in his thirties who looked pure and a woman who had an eye torn out and her jaw ripped off. Pop, pop, pop.

Cassie was drying Laura's feet with the towel. Laura was squirming, ticklish as ever. I left the rifle and climbed onto Mina's rock, sitting down behind her and putting my hands on her shoulders, feeling her breathe. The tide was receding quickly and clouds were rolling in. If we wanted to get home before dark we'd have to leave soon. I copied Mina and closed my eyes, listening to the sea. Laura screeched, making me jump. Cassie had stopped drying and started tickling. She was a merciless tickler; Laura wouldn't be left alone until she couldn't breathe, though in Laura's case this never took very long. "Eleven!" shouted Kyle. "She rides!"

The five of us were bone tired by the time we got home. I was yawning as I trudged into the house behind Kyle. I washed and changed, ready for bed, but it was only six o'clock so we piled a mound of whizz onto the coffee table. By ten to seven we were fresh as daisies and raring to go. Bradley surprised me by staying in the living room when Mina turned the music up and Cassie put pornography on. I suspected Bradley of an ulterior motive.

"Don't ask me about the zeds," I warned him when he turned to me. "We didn't see many today so I won't be able to answer any of your questions."

"You did a good job on the roof," Bradley told me. "Thank you for helping me, it would have taken much longer if I'd had to do it myself. It's good to see you have a head for heights."

I muttered thanks darkly.

"There's sand everywhere," complained Laura. She was painting her toenails sparkly blue. "We'll never get rid of it, it's going to stick around forever. In my hair, on my feet, in the bed. I hate it when it's in the bed." Laura looked up at the television and wrinkled her nose. "Why do they always have to come on the woman's face? It makes me feel sick."

"Those are the rules," explained Cassie.

"I think it's stupid," said Laura. I didn't think that Cassie was going to change Laura's mind on this one.

"You told us you wanted to be a Mr Man when you grew up," I said to Bradley. "Which one would you be?"

"Mr Small," said Laura, smiling.

"Mr Precocious," said Chloe, laughing.

"I'll probably end up as Mr Zed," answered Bradley sadly.

"Eleven," Kyle reminded us as he walked by.

More lines went around along with the gin. Cassie and Mina made a smiley face from whizz and vacuumed it up together. Laura clipped her ankle bracelet on and I stared at it until she told me to stop, it was freaking her out. I looked away with reluctance, ignoring Bradley's questions about foot fetishism. The cigarette smoke that clouded the room began to stifle me so I put on my coat and climbed the stairs to the attic where the rocket launcher stood. I

140

opened the doors and stepped out onto the balcony.

The ghost of the zed wail gave me an extra chill, doubly so when I pictured the City Centre and the river of zeds, all that dead light. Disappointing clouds were covering the sky, blanketing the stars and moon. The only things I could make out in the darkness were the three zeds moving in the street below. Two of them were together, the other was heading in their direction. The other was a naked man, glowing fiercely. The zed couple passed him by like he wasn't there. I heard someone behind me, picking their way through the lab. It was Chloe, enveloped in a huge coat with the hood pulled up, her hands lost in the pockets. The only feature I could really make out was her sharp nose. Chloe blew a few clouds of vapour and looked at the naked zed, who had stopped for some reason and was raising his hands like he was lifting something or, disturbingly, like he was gesturing to us.

"What's it doing?" Chloe asked me.

I shrugged. "Who knows why zeds do anything?"

The zed shook itself then carried on walking. It soon disappeared behind some trees. "We're going into town tomorrow," said Chloe, "it's time to find presents for Cassie."

I nodded and asked Chloe what she was going to get.

"I'll know when I see it," she said.

Travel with care, hunt places out, stand and shoot, smash and grab. Shopping for a loved one was never easy. Cassie hadn't been happy to be left at home but she hadn't been given any choice in the matter. We'd been gone for hours, it was mid afternoon now and only Laura's present was left. I was racing around another clothes shop with her and Mina, listening out for the jeep's horn that would tell us that the zeds were getting too close and we had to leave. It had happened in three other shops already today and each time had cut closer to the wire.

Laura paused, cocking her head, then she swept an armful of dresses from a rack as a zed tumbled down the stairs before us. Another one slid out of the dressing rooms. I shot one and Mina the other. The gunfire would draw more. We ran frantically for the door with Laura leading the way, a pistol in her free hand. Mina pushed her through the door where the others were waiting with the jeep. Before leaving I turned to look back at the shop. The zeds had come alive, their glow everywhere, at least twenty of them, all heading this way. The horn blasted twice and I jumped out into the street.

Relief swept through us all as Chloe drove home. Life near Zed City Centre was exciting but it was always nice to leave. The jeep was stuffed with our presents for Cassie. The dresses that Laura had just taken, weird shoes from Chloe, a Barbie make-up kit and hairbrush from Kyle, and a remote-controlled car from Bradley. Mina had taken a silk kimono, a gold cigarette lighter, and a ten inch black rubber strap-on dildo that I was sure Mina would quickly regret giving. I'd swiped a magnum of champagne, a tacky inflatable armchair to match the sex doll that Cassie had given me, and a diamond tiara that we almost couldn't get because the fucking jeweller's shop was so well protected. In the end Chloe had to ram-raid the place after we'd weakened the apparently titanium coated shutters with countless shotgun blasts.

Cassie was a nightmare for the next two days. She made an effort to control herself but it just wasn't in her nature. Her presents that we'd stored in the library were cattle-branded in her mind. What were they? How many? Were they funny or serious? Big or small? How big or small? Was she going to like them? What if she didn't? She'd know if she could take a quick peek, that's all she wanted, just a little look, that's all, it wouldn't ruin anything, it was her birthday after all, they were her presents, she had a right to do what she wanted and if we wouldn't let her she'd just have to take matters into her own hands.

Why had we locked the library door? Didn't we trust her? Did we know how hurtful that was? The library was empty! It was all a trick! She knew it all along, that's why she broke in, just to prove to us how devious we were, how we couldn't be trusted. She knew that the presents existed, she'd seen them in the back of the jeep, where had we hidden them? – *Come on Alex, look at me,* – *Come on Mina, I love you,* – *Come on Kyle, tell me and I'll let you...*

The darkness was total and I was having trouble breathing. My wrists were securely handcuffed to a ring above my head. I was naked and cold, trying to fight off memories of Walters and the truck. Kyle was opposite me a few metres away, in exactly the same position as I was, not that I could see him with this hood over my head and the lights turned out. Some surprise present for Cassie this was turning out to be.

It had been that genius Mina's idea. The party was in full swing when she'd taken us into a corner and offered her brilliant suggestion. I'd been whizzing and drunk, still was, so I'd said, "Yes, why not? Anything for the birthday girl." Kyle had agreed too so Mina took us down to the basement where she stripped us, cuffed us, hooded us and blew us before running back up the steps and turning out the light, leaving us alone with the zeds. I didn't know how long ago this had happened, maybe half an hour. Time passed differently down here in the basement.

Cassie had been overjoyed with her presents, particularly the kimono and the tiara. After everything had

143

been opened Cassie popped the champagne in the garden and we proceeded to get drunk and have fun with the remote-controlled car. Bradley used it to chase Laura around the grass until she ran back into the house. We all followed and at noon we started on the whizz. Cassie tried on all her new clothes and the weird shoes from Chloe. I used a pump to blow up the inflatable armchair then I put it in the corner of the living room. Mina and Chloe spelt out Happy Birthday in whizz on the coffee table, challenging Cassie to snort it all and make a wish. She raced around the words with a rolled up note then closed her eyes and whispered something with whizzy tears spilling down her cheeks.

The afternoon rushed by as we whizzed, talked and danced. Same with the evening. Bradley disappeared at some point but I couldn't remember when. At around ten o'clock Mina had come up with her fantastic idea and now here I was with Kyle, just waiting, handcuffed not a metre away from Kaylan. Kyle was next to Marian. I jumped away as a cold zed foot touched mine. The drawstring on the black silk hood was a constant pressure on my throat, gentle but slowly constricting. As well as the odd rattle of chains I could hear music coming from upstairs and the occasional peal of laughter.

"Fuck!" said Kyle. "How much longer can they be? This is fucking typical."

"You need to calm down," I said, telling this to myself as much as to Kyle.

"Fuck that. I want out." Kyle rattled his handcuffs pointlessly. "I can feel this fucking zed looking at me, Alex, I can fucking *feel* it. Wait till I get out of here, I'll kill Mina. Wait and fucking see."

The basement door opened, letting more of the music from upstairs in. The light was switched on and I heard two or three pairs of feet coming down the steps. At last.

Kyle immediately began shouting but I knew it wouldn't do any good so I kept quiet. People were moving over the carpet.

"Mina, you shouldn't have." The voice was Cassie's. "All this for me?"

"I've been hanging here for hours!" wailed Kyle. "Get these fucking things off me!"

"Shame you didn't gag him," mentioned Cassie. "Well boys, aren't you going to sing me Happy Birthday?"

"We've done that already," snapped Kyle. "Get the key, Mina. Let us down. Please."

Mina just laughed, and I think I heard Laura laughing too.

"You bitches!" Kyle was sounding angrier by the second. He rattled his handcuffs furiously and I heard him slamming himself against the wall.

"See if you can't calm him down, Mina," said Cassie. Suddenly Kyle stopped moving and for about twenty seconds the only sounds around us were those made by the zeds. I wondered what they were making of all this. "There you are," said Cassie. "Mina, you carry on with Kyle. Laura, come with me." I held my breath and closed my eyes until I felt someone scrape hard fingernails slowly down my chest.

Chapter 9

There weren't many cars on this particular stretch of motorway due to the old police block that we'd passed a mile back. The cars that were around were parked along the hard shoulder, most of them looking like they'd been parked in a hurry. Kyle had found a battered megaphone on the road. He tried speaking through it but it didn't work anymore. There were plenty of zeds about, nicely scattered in all directions. The two long swords ("It's called a *katana*," Bradley always insisted, but no one listened) had been claimed by Mina and Kyle. On a whim I'd decided to bring the aluminium baseball bat, and now I was glad that I did. It felt good to use the old weapon again, the thing had sentimental value. Cassie had saved my life with it, and I'd used it to kill my first zed. You couldn't guarantee that a zed would stay down after you'd whacked it but then this random element appealed to me.

The closest zed was wearing a gory shirt and a suit that had turned to mush in the rain. I whacked the bat into the zed's stomach then slammed it over the back of its head. The zed fell and lay still. I hit it again to make sure, splitting its skull as someone began shooting behind me. The next zed was dressed in overalls and heavy boots, thick hair hiding much of its eyes. I wound the bat up and let fly when the zed was in range. The bat cracked the zed's chin beautifully, sending a shockwave through my body and caving the zed's jaw back into its head. I hefted the bat and checked its dents, impressed once again by the damage it could do.

Mina called to us and waved. She pointed at the hill

behind her and disappeared down the embankment, the rest of us following, collecting rifles on the way. We waded through the grass and up the hill after Mina, watching her run up the grassy slope, her arms pumping. She reached the crown of trees at the top and waved again, then she did a few cartwheels and a somersault.

The top of the hill was covered in drying leaves. We cleared a space where we could sit and look down over the motorway. The grass was springy and dry, the green view exhilarating. Kyle took a rifle and climbed the easiest looking tree. He lay across one of the overhanging branches and began scanning the road for zeds. Laura picked up my rifle and lay on her stomach, sighting carefully. I was resting against a tree with Cassie, my arms and shoulders beginning to ache from the fun I'd had with the bat. Mina sat cross legged a metre away, tucking her hair behind her ears.

"I see you," said Kyle. Crack, a distant zed fell and lay twisted on the road, adding to the bodies that were already there.

"This is so peaceful," said Mina. "I never did this kind of thing before the zeds came along. The quiet, the trees, everything. It's a shame Chloe's missing this, I'm sure she'd like it."

Kyle shifted awkwardly in the tree. "You're wrong," he said. "Chloe's a city girl, she'd hate it here. The countryside fucks her up, all these open spaces."

Laura's rifle spat a bullet and another zed went down.

"These cigarettes are getting stale," Cassie said, lighting one up. "It won't be long before they're all too dry, they'll disappear in one drag. We have to make the most of them while we can."

I saw Cassie's point and lit one myself. Kyle's tree had begun to creak ominously. I tried thinking of what Bradley would say if he'd been here but I couldn't think of anything, except for his possible complaint that you could see right up Laura's skirt from here. Cassie seemed to notice this, too.

"Who brought the whizz?" she said suddenly.

I took one of Chloe's wraps from my jacket and held it up between finger and thumb. Laura shot a zed as we debated how we were going to do the lines. What we needed was a flat surface. Cassie came up with the idea of using Mina's stomach. Mina laughed and lay on the grass, pulling up her top. "Don't breathe too deeply," warned Cassie as she tapped the whizz out over Mina's skin. Both rifles cracked simultaneously and Cassie's hand jerked. "Fuck," she whispered.

"Your hands are cold," hissed Mina.

Cassie asked if we were all having some. Laura and Kyle refused, staying with their guns. Cassie cut four lines and we shared them between us, licking up the remnants when we were done. Mina unwisely decided to cut one long line on the back of Laura's leg. She tipped some whizz over the back of Laura's knee and started in with a credit card. Within a few seconds Laura was giggling and just as Mina had the line ready Laura's leg twitched involuntarily and the whizz was lost in the grass. Mina sighed and did her lines on Cassie instead.

We soon ran into some trouble. Everything seemed fine, we were just chatting away as Laura and Kyle played sharpshooters when Mina stretched herself out on her back and found herself looking up at a huge fucking zed. She rolled and yelled as the zed swiped at her, missing by centimetres. I jumped up with Cassie, shouting at Kyle to shoot while Cassie went for the spare rifle. There were other zeds amongst the trees, I could see their glow flitting around between the treetrunks and branches. Mina scrambled towards us and I pulled her to her feet, then I heard wood snap and Kyle fell out of the tree, hitting the ground hard, lying there winded as four zeds moved in. Pop, pop, pop, pop. The zeds fell as if by magic, a red laser spot appearing on their faces before their heads blew out. I turned and there was Laura down on one knee, the rifle at her shoulder. She'd had to shoot past us to kill the zeds, it must have been fucking close.

"Very nice," said Cassie appreciatively. She helped Kyle to his feet and Mina kicked the zed that had nearly taken hold of her. She turned back to us with her hands covering her face. I gave her a hug and Kyle picked up his rifle in an embarrassed way, trying and failing to crack a smile. Laura tidied up her hair, brushed the leaves from her jacket and started down the hill back to the road.

Bradley's bedroom was in messy contrast to his library. It was strewn with random piles of clothes and plates, a tangle of sheets, books, disks, CDs, notebooks, videotapes and, for some reason, six pillows. The wardrobe, full of superhero T-shirts, stood with its doors hanging open. The stereo was on the dresser, playing tacky pop music again. I didn't know why Bradley listened to this stuff. On the desk was a computer and a lamp. The monitor was showing a brightly coloured pie chart. Next to the keyboard was an open textbook that was covered in Bradley's notes. The boy in question had gone to make a sandwich, sandwiches being Bradley's staple diet. I was sitting on the bed with a bottle of wine that was nearly empty. I heard someone whooping then Cassie ran past the open door with Mina in hot pursuit. Not long after that Bradley came back, with what I suspected was a peanut butter, pickle and mustard sandwich. He was wearing his Mr Freeze T-shirt and looked vaguely surprised to see me still here.

"Hello," I said, "hello." This was my second bottle of wine. "Tell me more about the graphs and stuff."

Bradley took his chair and did something with the mouse. The picture changed to a jagged red line across the screen. "I'm just gathering data," he told me, putting his plate on the desk. "There's nothing to tell. The project isn't working out the way I hoped it would." Bradley began eating his sandwich with a forlorn expression. "The only thing I can say is that the zeds are unpredictable, but we already knew that." His words were garbled around his food. "I'll continue to input data, see what I come up with. It's as good a way as any to pass the time and it's comforting to know that something about the zeds is being recorded, even if nothing can be learned from it."

We heard Cassie shouting from the living room. "No! Bitch! Give it back!" Someone was running through the hall. Laura burst into Bradley's room with Cassie's tiara on her head. She jumped over the bed and hid herself under a pile of blankets. Cassie poked her head around the door. "Which way did she go? Is she in here? She is, isn't she?" Cassie got her answer as Laura failed to suppress a giggle. Cassie launched herself at the biggest lump under the sheets but she became entangled and suddenly Laura was out. She bounced over the bed and as Cassie fought to free herself Laura stopped to wiggle in the doorway, posing with the tiara and saying, "It looks much better on me, anyone can see that." Cassie roared and tore the blankets away. The chase was on again.

"We're getting the heating installed tomorrow," said Bradley. "I'm tired of being cold, it makes me slow."

"What's the plan?" I asked.

"You'll see. It may not be practical and I'm sure there's a better solution but it'll just have to do." Bradley started the second half of his sandwich, then looked at it carefully. "This bread tastes so much better than the pasty dough I used to get in the shops. I didn't know any better back then."

There were the sounds of running feet again. As soon as Laura came into view she crashed to the floor with Cassie on top of her. The tiara flew from Laura's head and lay sparkling on the carpet. "Ha!" cried Cassie triumphantly. "Now you're going to pay."

Laura was struggling bravely but there was no way out with Cassie on her back. I swallowed some wine and Bradley took another bite of his sandwich as Cassie sent her fingers fluttering at Laura's face. Laura, knowing what was coming, struggled even harder. "No!" she howled. "Help!"

Cassie laughed, swooping her fingers past Laura's bulging eyes, then she dug her fingers into Laura's sides. Laura screamed with hellish laughter, thrashing and kicking the carpet. Cassie tickled her again and Laura's screams rose high enough to shatter glass, then to knock down walls. After another tickle, and another, Laura's face was purple, half dead. Only then did Cassie release her, standing up and reclaiming the tiara. She slipped it over her head.

"You're wrong," Cassie said. "It looks better on *me*." With that she walked away. Laura was lying motionless, hands like claws, tense as a wire. She moved her toes first, then she collapsed into the carpet and started coughing. I drank the last of the wine and Bradley finished his sandwich as we watched Laura's face move slowly from purple to pink. She opened bloodshot eyes and heaved herself up from the floor. Still coughing, Laura slunk away, clutching her sides.

Bradley shook his head. "It's terrible to see what one human being can do to another," he said.

This was our first warm weekend for over a month. Every room that needed it had heating but, as Bradley had warned, the method wasn't the most practical. Chloe had parked the flatbed truck outside and we'd all helped to move the gas fires into the house. Next came the canisters, horribly heavy and difficult to grip. Chloe moved the truck into next door's driveway with most of the canisters still on board. We covered them with a tarpaulin then closed the tall gate. The time would come when all the canisters would be empty, then we'd have to back to the yard to collect some more. It wasn't an infinite supply of heat but it was all we had. Long term thinking wasn't too big with us anyway, not with all the fucking zeds out there.

The windows around the house misted up quickly, providing an extra comfort barrier between us and the zed world outside. I lazed about the living room in T-shirt and jeans, drinking bourbon with Kyle and watching Bradley's Bogart movies. Cassie, Laura and Mina were holed up in the bedroom. Over the months that we'd lived here the three girls' periods had somehow synchronised so that they all came on at roughly the same time, give or take a day. Right now the girls were lying in bed in their pyjamas, along with a bowlful of downers and a vast array of cigarettes, magazines, chocolate and crisps.

"What's going on?" Kyle wanted to know. "Who's killed who?"

I could only shrug in answer before finishing my drink. Chloe didn't even look up from the book she was reading. She might have raised an eyebrow but I couldn't be sure. I sloshed more bourbon into my glass and continued in my attempt to watch the movie. We wouldn't be going out for a few days so it was important for me to get into the quieter things in life.

"Fuck all this," said Kyle. "I'm bored. It's only eight o'clock."

"Have another drink," I said, tossing Kyle the bottle.

"I'll have one too," put in Chloe. She left her book and lit a cigarette in an elegant kind of way that she'd picked up from the women in the Bogart movies, maybe this very one we were watching now. Or was this the first time we'd seen it? Kyle poured the drinks and we watched the screen in silence until Bradley walked in wearing his Fantastic Four T-shirt.

"It's time to move on," he announced, flopping down on the floor close to the fire. "Bogart is beginning to pale, Casablanca being the obvious exception. Our lives here are inevitably static but this doesn't have to mean that our tastes must follow suit. We need new heroes, new dreams."

Kyle sneered. "We? All this black and white shit bores me to death. It's only on because we've seen everything else five thousand times."

"That's precisely my point," said Bradley.

I threw a cushion at him, managing to hit him on the head. "So, Mr Fantastic," I said, "who's going to be your new hero?"

"Cagney," answered Bradley, using the cushion to make himself more comfortable.

Chloe was confused. "Cagney? Who's he?"

The movie finished after another twenty minutes. It took us another twenty to finish the bottle, Chloe becoming the drunkest of us. She was kissing Kyle, talking in a low voice and laughing in a loud one. I took a bottle of water from the fridge and drank some on my way to the bedroom. The girls were still up, hazy on the pills. They waved at me in slow motion as I undressed. I cleared away some of the crisp packets and chocolate wrappers then jumped into bed next to Cassie, who was holding her stomach and smoking a cigarette. Mina was trying to read an upside down magazine with Laura leaning over her shoulder.

"To the top of the world," I said, already drifting to sleep.

"Whus tha?" asked one of the girls, I couldn't tell who.

The flying bullets marked the beginning of a new week. Kyle blasted the shotgun and blew a zed through a window in the videostore. Cassie jumped up onto the roof of the jeep and sprayed the car park with the machine gun. The monster food and clothing shops surrounding us were hundreds of metres away. There were hordes of zeds around but by the time they reached here we'd be long gone. Bradley was running towards us, pushing a shopping trolley before him. I picked off a zed that was in his way. Bradley made a war face and charged into the videostore, Mina and Kyle behind him. I turned to shoot more zeds, hearing bullets tear into glowing skin or ricochet off concrete and brick, listening to Cassie scream insults, my vision confined to the sights and the zeds at the end of them.

The wind was beginning to whip itself up as I lowered my rifle and took a short rest. There weren't any trees around but leaves were blowing in all directions. One of them got caught in Laura's hair when she was slapping a new clip into the Uzi. I noticed that the zeds were forming into groups in the neighbouring car parks, each group at least a hundred strong. Some of the zeds closer to us were retreating to join them but most flowed blindly on until they caught bullets in their heads.

Chloe was standing at the open door of the jeep, her rifle poking through the window. She saw something then ducked into the jeep and slammed the door. Bradley and the others were back with the trolley, now bulging with tapes and DVDs. The rest of us moved closer and Kyle helped Bradley load up. Cassie slid herself off the roof and crawled onto the back seat. We followed her, leaving the rusting trolley to the zeds.

The closest group was moving in steadily. Chloe turned the jeep towards them then slowed right down as she drove us through the car park exit. The zeds were only a few metres away now. Laura sat in the front seat, Mina had the window. The two girls took their guns and leaned outside then pulled the triggers, bullets slicing through the zeds as Chloe drove on by. When we reached the roundabout the fun was over. We drove away with ears ringing, the car park behind us piled with bodies, running with zed blood. It felt good to leave a mark, to make a difference.

Bradley soon began a tedious conversation with Chloe about the jeep's engine. He thought it needed to be looked at. Chloe thought it was running fine. Bradley disagreed and pointed out the possibly fatal danger of breakdown. Chloe took his point but warned Bradley about what she called his encroaching paranoia. I laughed at that, as did Laura. Bradley looked cross and began a lecture on the aesthetic principle of living dangerously weighed against the mediocrity of foolhardy short-sightedness. Mina rolled her eyes and Kyle pretended to fall asleep. Cassie seemed lost somewhere, staring into her lap. Before Bradley could finish Chloe caved in and agreed to help him when we got home.

The double garage was always kept meticulously clean. Our bikes stood against the wall and the ghost smell of grass cuttings could still be detected in the air. Our jeep, lit harshly by the flourescents above, was parked with Chloe looking bored behind the wheel. Bradley was busy with the engine, oil up to his elbows, turning constantly to the open textbook at his side. He'd been forced to stand on his toolbox to get a better view of what he was doing. I found myself surprised by how dull this experience was. After making a couple of token circles around the jeep I left for the kitchen, looking back to see Chloe watching me with a viciously raised eyebrow.

Cassie was cutting out whizz on the kitchen table and telling Kyle that she wanted to go outside. He grunted distantly as he inspected his handgun. I was about to sit down for a line when Cassie asked me to find Laura and Mina. Cassie looked strange; withdrawn, serious even. I found the living room empty and moved to the bedroom. The girls were there, Mina sitting lightly over Laura's face, Mina's hands back against the headboard, eyes closed, the tip of her tongue perched delicately on her upper lip. I watched for ten seconds then retreated into the hall and back to the kitchen.

"They're busy," I said.

"Busy fucking I suppose," muttered Cassie, "that's all they do these days." She snorted two gigantic lines and grabbed an unopened bottle of vodka from the freezer. A thin film of ice had formed around it. "I'm going out now," Cassie told us, unscrewing the bottle, "come with me if you want." She threw her head back and gulped some vodka then whacked the bottle on the table and shuddered. After exchanging a look with Kyle I filled up on whizz then took a swallow. Kyle did the same. Looking pleased, Cassie took the bottle and one of the pistols from the table. "There's hours of light left," she said, "let's go and enjoy it. Forget the rifle, Alex, the pistol will do. Grab another bottle and we'll go."

It was colder than I expected outside and the autumn light was stark and hard, like zed light. We followed Cassie down the driveway and out through the gate. It snicked grimly shut behind us. There were no zeds in sight, at least not yet. I didn't like this one bit. I was whizzing, which was fine, but I was getting drunk too, and we only had handguns. What was the point of this? We drank more vodka, passing the bottles around.

"Where are we going?" asked Kyle.

"Nowhere," answered Cassie. She started walking down the street, the bottle and the gun dangling carelessly from her hands.

"What the fuck's her problem?" Kyle hissed at me.

"I haven't *got* a fucking problem," Cassie said loudly. "If you don't want to come, fuck off. Both of you."

Kyle laughed like it was all a joke. I caught up with Cassie and took a few more swallows. The drink was tasteless and the kick it gave made me feel stronger. I took another gulp as we turned a corner where someone's jeep had crashed into a tree. The windscreen was cracked where the driver's head had probably smashed into it. Kyle trotted up to us and pointed down the road. Zeds were moving there, two of them coming for us, three walking away. We killed them when we got close enough. Cassie looked closely at the bodies, three women and two men. Their brains were leaking out onto the street. Kyle opened his mouth to say something then shut it again. I realised that I hadn't brought any cigarettes.

As we continued to walk we continued to drink, the two bottles going around in silence. I was more unsteady all the time but the whizz in my system was keeping me frosty. The zeds were dotted around in various places. We didn't shoot many of them. Kyle put a hand on Cassie's shoulder but she shrugged it off and said something under her breath. We took turns at random, quickly losing ourselves. I felt sure that we weren't going to make it back, but I was with Cassie, and since the zeds came we were all living on borrowed time anyway. It had to run out sooner or later.

The light was fading and the last bottle was nearly empty when Cassie held up her hand and stopped. No one had spoken for over an hour. We waited, swaying on our feet. The houses around us were impressive but their security was poor. Cassie opened the nearest gate and we walked up the wide driveway that led to the house. Barren trees overhung left and right. The garden was choked with leaves. A zed was standing beneath one of the trees, watching us. Cassie turned and strode towards it. The zed was somewhere in his twenties with a shaved head, wearing jeans and a black jacket that was pasted with leaves. The zed didn't move as we approached. Its eyes didn't flicker as Cassie walked up to it, put her gun to its forehead and pulled the trigger. The zed flopped onto the grass. Cassie finished the bottle and threw it away. She closed her eyes then took off her jacket and pulled her jeans off over her trainers. Cassie got on all fours next to the zed and called us over, rolling her underwear down to her thighs. She turned her head to us and told Kyle to fuck her.

"What?" Kyle took a step back. "No way, I can't."

Cassie was in no mood for argument. "Just do it, Kyle. Fuck me."

Kyle looked confused as he took off his clothes and positioned himself behind Cassie. "Not there," she snapped as he was about to start, "here." Cassie spread her ass, spitting on her fingers, pushing them in to lubricate herself. Kyle, after looking at me in a despairing way, began pushing his cock inside. Cassie gritted her teeth and closed her eyes, gun still in her hand. The dead zed was staring up at the branches, the intensity gone from its eyes. The glow was still there but it was just starting to fade. Kyle was looking at his dick going in and out of Cassie's ass, obviously wanting to get this over with as quickly as he could. Then Cassie started to cry and put a tender hand on the zed's shining neck. I bit my lip, filled with dread about Cassie asking me to fuck her next. All too quickly Kyle grimaced and tipped his head back to the sky. He froze for a second then pulled out and moved away.

Cassie was adamant through her tears and within a

minute I'd taken over from Kyle. Cassie started sobbing, caressing the zed's face, turning its head to hers, pushing her ass back hard. I held her hips and Cassie kissed the zed, sliding her tongue into its slack mouth. I focused on what I was doing and at last I started to come. Cassie's body was shaking as she cried, her tears falling into the zed's eyes. She put her gun to its head and blasted the side of its skull open. She shot it again and its teeth flew out through its cheek. As I came Cassie pushed the smoking gun deep into her mouth, moaning loudly. I was paralysed, convinced that she was going to pull the trigger and that would be it, game over. Instead Cassie pulled the gun out and threw up messily over the zed's ruined face.

The light was almost gone and the fatalism that had previously comforted me had worn away. I wanted to live, fuck all that borrowed time. We sat around in the garden while Cassie recovered. She wouldn't talk and kept her back turned to us, rocking herself with her arms locked around her chest. I was trying to discuss with Kyle about how the hell we were going to get out of this. Our orgasms had drained us of energy and the whizz was starting to wear off, but we were feeling more drunk with every breath. Positive thinking was difficult.

"I think there's only two things we can do," I said to Kyle, both of us watching Cassie. "We can try to make it home right now, which would be stupid, or we can hide in the house until morning, which would be smart. What do you think?"

"We'll hide in the house," said Kyle, scrubbing his cheek. "I feel like stir fried shit. My head, my throat. All I need is a glass of water. One fucking glass."

"You'll get it tomorrow," I said, putting an arm around his shoulders.

"I'll be fucking dead by tomorrow if I don't get a

drink."

There was no point delaying any longer. I crawled over to Cassie and told her the plan. She nodded and got to her feet, wiping her mouth with her sleeve. We checked our guns and moved to the back of the house. A foul-smelling pond was the centrepiece of the garden. The door was locked so we had to break in. This obviously meant that zeds could get in too but they'd have to open the gate first, then come round to the back. The chances were on our side. Our biggest problem was searching the house. The only thing I felt fit for was passing out. Going on a zed hunt before I could do so wasn't going to be fun at all.

As we stood in the kitchen preparing ourselves we heard something moving behind one of the doors. Sliding footsteps, fingernails scraping wood. A door swung open and there was a little zed in the hallway, dressed in pyjamas. It wasted no time in coming for us. I shot it through the nose, blood and brains spattering on the hard floor like vomit before the zed went down. We stepped over the body and checked the other rooms. We found a crawler in the dining room and a baby zed on the stairs. An old zed was waiting on the landing. Cassie didn't do any shooting, she just trailed behind us with a vacant look on her face.

The master bedroom was a mess, sheets torn up and blood everywhere, there were even splashes on the ceiling. The little zed's room was scattered with dusty toys. The cot in the nursery was full of old blood. The last zed we found was locked in a wardrobe. We heard it thumping around inside before we riddled the doors with bullets. One of them fell off and the zed tumbled out, torn up but still on line. Kyle finished it off and we climbed into the last room, the attic. It had been converted into a bedsit, posters covering the walls, a birdcage with a feathery skeleton inside it. The wide bed was stale and dusty but it would have to do. We shook out the sheets and pillows, choking clouds of dust making our eyes water. When we'd made the bed we rolled into it, leaving our guns under the pillows for easy access. The window in the roof showed some stars beginning to shine. Now that I was resting, the headache that had been looming began to chainsaw its way around my brain. The dehydration was even worse. I put an arm around Cassie and kissed her hair. Kyle's arm was resting across her hips. Cassie was looking at the sloping ceiling.

"Today was a special anniversary for me." Her voice was a crone's. "Don't ask me anything about it. Don't discuss it with anyone else." I kissed her again, thinking that a zed could walk in at any moment.

Dawn took us out of an uneasy sleep. The three of us groaned simultaneously and covered our eyes. My headache was just about bearable, the problem lay in the thirst. My first thought was of water, the essence of life, the purest of the pure. Odourless, colourless, tasteless. My second thought was of obtaining water, an impossibly elysian dream. I ground my teeth in despair and tried to get back to sleep.

Cassie herded us downstairs and out into the garden. We sucked the dew from the grass for what could have been half an hour. It gave us temporary respite. We hopped about to warm ourselves up and discussed how we'd find the easiest route home. The one positive factor was that we had plenty of bullets. The negative factors would have to take care of themselves. Then Cassie, who was almost her old self again, clapped her hands in surprise.

"We're so fucking stupid," she said. "We don't have to find our way home, we just need to get ourselves noticed. They're bound to be out looking for us soon, they know we couldn't have gone far. We'll build a fire, put some smoky stuff on it, then we just wait."

The zeds began to flock as soon as the fire was smoking properly. As well as the tyre we found in the garage we used plenty of clothes and sheets, old newspapers and a pile of wood, liberally dosed with kerosene. The fire was set in the middle of the road. After lighting it we watched from the upstairs window. A zed in flannel trousers stumbled too close to the flames and began to smoulder. Another one in a nightdress tried the same trick and went up like a torch. The craze spread quickly and before very long there were eight or nine burning zeds staggering around the street. Under different circumstances we'd have found the whole thing pretty funny.

The fire had been burning for well over an hour before the jeep turned up. We cheered as Chloe jammed on the brakes and Bradley began taking down the zeds with his machine gun. Kyle grabbed a metal folding chair that was leaning against the wall and hurled it through the window. Bradley waved but Chloe ignored us. We took our pistols and hurried outside, taking potshots at the zeds as we crossed the driveway. By the time we reached the gates there were none left standing.

"You must have quite a tale to tell," Bradley said, opening the back door and ushering us inside the jeep. He scuttled to the front and joined Chloe. There was an inviting looking plastic bag at our feet. Kyle opened it and took out three large bottles of crystal clear water that danced with twinkles from the early morning sun. We scrabbled eagerly to drink what we could as Chloe turned us around and headed for home. The withered sponges of our bodies sucked up the water with relish. In what seemed like a very short time the bottles were empty. I was

162

starting to feel sick again. Kyle was wincing, clutching his stomach. Cassie burped and tossed her bottle out of the window.

"One of you should know how to drive," scolded Chloe, her eyes flicking angrily at us in the rear-view mirror. "It could have saved us all this trouble. And did you think about Laura and Mina? They're going out of their minds. They didn't come home until dark last night, and they left today at dawn, looking for you. They could be anywhere by now, they could be *dead*. All you had to do is tell someone where you were going."

Cassie giggled behind her hand. I caught her eyes and couldn't help starting too. Kyle spluttered and we all burst into laughter, Cassie rocking back in her seat, pointing at Chloe and howling. Chloe gripped the wheel tight and said something that was probably insulting. We laughed harder and joined hands, catching the attention of the odd zed as we drove by. Bradley turned and cocked his head at us, grave and questioning as usual but this time mercifully silent.

It was getting dark again by the time Laura and Mina came home. They crashed into the living room where I was sitting with Cassie and Bradley, watching a Cagney movie. Chloe and Kyle had disappeared long ago. When Laura saw Cassie she started crying in an angry kind of way and my heart sank. Mina carefully put one hand on her hip, the other on Laura's shoulder. Mina's face was stormier than I could ever have imagined. Cassie squeezed my knee then stood up and smiled her most winning smile. She held out her arms. "Did you miss me?" she asked over Laura's sobs.

"Bedroom," said Mina, jerking her thumb back over her shoulder. Cassie paused dubiously, took another look at Mina's face, then she sighed and walked slowly out of the room. Laura was following close behind. Now Mina was looking at me. I squirmed under her gaze, trying to find something to say. It occurred to me that I'd made a mistake in not interrupting Mina and Laura while they were fucking. I jumped when Laura suddenly screamed, "*You cold cunt fucking bitch!*" There was a dull thud and Cassie cried out in pain. Mina looked at me again before shutting the door and leaving me with Bradley.

"And I'd thought the twenties were roaring," he said.

"What?"

"Nothing. It seems like you're the only one who's escaping punishment over this spontaneous action."

"I suppose so," I shrugged, hearing someone being thrown to the floor in the bedroom and Laura screaming again.

Bradley plucked at his Silver Surfer T-shirt. "Existence is a spontaneous process," he told me. "The best way to experience it is through a *dance*. Don't feel too bad."

I nodded knowingly but I was confused about the movie. "Which one is Cagney?" I asked.

Chapter 10

The seven of us were crowded around the two fires in the living room, most of us drinking coffee. Mina had hot chocolate, Bradley a glass of water. It was early afternoon but the featureless sky outside made things darker than they should have been. The fires hissed efficiently, making the air above them ripple. Cassie's black eye had finally healed. Her split lip had been puffy for a couple of days but now the only mark left was a small cut. Laura had been dragged off Cassie by Mina. She'd been held to the floor for nearly five minutes before she'd stopped struggling. Since then things had been gradually thawing out and I thought that we were almost back to normal. A trip outside would add the finishing touch, or even a visit to the basement. No one had been down there since the fight, except to make routine checks on the chains that held our zeds in place.

"It's story time," announced Cassie, breaking our long silence.

"What's the story about?" asked Mina, breathing in the steam from her hot chocolate.

Cassie sipped her coffee. "The story's about how we killed our first zed. We've never talked about that before. Who wants to start?"

"I killed mine with a car," Chloe told us. "Do you remember that Mercedes? I'd been driving with two people I'd picked up, we needed petrol. Zeds were absolutely everywhere, and they all looked so *hungry*. One of them jumped up on the bonnet when I was turning a corner. It was old, thirtysomething, a business woman I think, nice suit. I didn't know what to do. Patrick told me to blow the horn and I laughed. The zed was holding onto the wipers, biting the glass, smearing its lipstick. Annie shook me and told me to brake, so I did. The zed flew, the wipers were still in its hands. When it stopped rolling it sat up and started to crawl on its knees, looking at me. I just floored it. We hit the zed and some of its teeth bounced off the windscreen. Then we reached the petrol station. Annie and Patrick, well, the zeds got them. Annie was looking right at me when they killed her."

"I used my sister's hockey stick," said Kyle, smiling. He hung his arm around Chloe. "There was a gang of us, twenty people, all ages. Laura was there, but she wouldn't talk to anyone, they thought she was nuts. Anyway, this gang didn't last long. Best weapons we had were flare guns, can you believe that? The zeds caught up with us, hundreds of the fuckers. We didn't have a chance. It was pissing with rain and this zed was facing me, little cunt with glasses. I smacked him with the stick but I swear he didn't even feel it so I hit him as hard as I could, it wasn't easy to bring yourself to do that back then, that kind of thing takes some getting used to. *Crack!* He went down and started to have a fit or some shit, so I hit him again and the fucking stick broke in half, but the zed stopped moving. He was dead. Trouble is, so was everyone else, except for Laura. She was shooting zeds with the flare gun, and she was *laughing*. Was that your first time?"

"No." Laura lit another cigarette. "I was waiting in my house, I thought the police would come. After a while someone started banging on the front window. I heard it break and I ran downstairs. It was my mum. She was a zed now, all cut up by the glass. I ran back out into the garden. Mr Eliot was waiting there."

"The dance instructor," I said. "The one with the hard-on."

Laura nodded. "Our back wall was falling down. I tried climbing over it and it collapsed. I grabbed one of the bricks before Mr Eliot could get me. I smashed him in the face with it and he fell down. He started to get up so I got another brick and hit the side of his head with it. Blood and some other stuff squirted out of his ears. Then I saw my mum, she was coming towards me like she wanted a hug. I ran away."

"I was lucky my dad had a gun," said Mina. "The first time I used it was to kill a zed. It was easy, I just opened the window and pulled the trigger."

"Mine was easy too," I said. "Cassie saved me in this church with the baseball bat. When we went outside we saw a zed walking up the path through the graveyard. Cassie handed me the bat and told me to kill it. It felt good."

Bradley lay back on the carpet and closed his eyes. "The first zed I killed was right outside our house. Mrs Buxton, the dressmaker. She baked wonderful cakes, I remember having one shaped like a spaceship for my ninth birthday. To kill her I used my father's power drill. As a close quarters weapon it was extremely effective. Through the eyeball or, if the zed was much taller than me, under the chin or beneath the ear. Mrs Buxton was a little shorter than I am. After drilling her I didn't have the time to reflect on how I felt as my father was calling me from the front door. He was in plaster at the time and he couldn't get his wheelchair over the step. He became so angry that he fell out of the chair and onto the pavement, hitting his head and knocking himself unconscious."

We all sniggered and Bradley opened his eyes. Cassie pushed her hair back away from her face. "I was in town, I had to get home," she said. "I needed to find my mother to see if she was all right. It was dark, people were running away from the zeds but there was nowhere to go. I saw a car-crash, one car went through the lights and everyone was screaming, then it hit another one and they spun right into the crowd, hundreds of people. There were bodies everywhere, people dying, fires, it was like hell.

"I started running again, fighting my way through, then someone pushed me and I thought I was going to fall. This man caught me and started feeling my tits, the sick bastard. He pushed me against the wall and I kicked him in the balls. I ran into an alley, you know, where they sold those weird fish. It was really dark. People were looting the shops and the alarms were going crazy but there was no one around in the alleyway so I started running again until I saw the zed in front of me. It was kneeling on the floor, biting someone. I slipped in the blood and fell over the body, skinned my knee, my elbow. The zed spat something out and took a hold of my ankle. I kicked it in the face and tried to get away but the ground was too slippery and the zed kept coming.

"Something snapped then and I got mad. I jumped at the zed and grabbed it around the neck. I was kneeling in the body on the floor, squelching in the blood. The zed was moaning with its hands up my skirt. I pulled the zed up and whacked its head on the floor. It didn't have any effect so I did it again, harder, but the zed was still moving, still feeling me up. Then I lost it, I don't know exactly what happened but when I got up the zed wasn't moving anymore and I had brains running over my hands."

Shopping was rarely much fun when there was no whizz to make us brave, and the expedition on Thursday was no exception. The blank, wet weather didn't help much either. We were bickering about which place we should hit when Chloe threw her hands up in frustration and parked at the first supermarket we came across. It was left to Chloe and Kyle to stand in the rain while the rest of us went inside. I was shivering inside my jacket, stumbling about the place with the others, choosing food at random. I couldn't wait to get back to the house, back to the warmth and the light that was waiting there.

A sudden burst of machine gun fire made me wince and I dropped the jar I was holding. It bounced on the floor but didn't break. We turned into the next aisle to find a small group of zeds, five of them. We stopped moving and I shuffled my feet, looking away and listening to the rain outside. The zeds waited passively. Bradley raised his gun then lowered it again. He opened his mouth, an expectant look on his face, then he sneezed loudly. I tried to catch Cassie's eye but she was watching the floor. Laura pushed me aside and approached the zeds, raising the shotgun. Five blasts and the zeds were down. Bradley sneezed again and we continued with the shopping

Chloe drove us home quicker than usual, probably because she'd got soaked in the rain. The girls spent the journey gazing out of their respective windows. When we got home we unpacked and lit the fires, Chloe and Kyle leaving for their bedroom to change. I helped Bradley in the kitchen, making crisp sandwiches for everyone. Bradley complained constantly about his cold. We all ate our sandwiches together in the living room, watching a sci-fi movie about a supercomputer gone bad.

After food we smoked cigarettes and started on the tequila. It wasn't long before I was feeling better about the day. The shopping was done, I had a pleasant buzz growing in my head, the rain may have been battering the windows but in here it was warm and dry, if a little smoky. The movie was terrible but you couldn't have everything. Chloe left the room and headed for the attic to get the whizz ready, which was good news. It was only half past twelve and I didn't feel up to drinking all day.

"This film is shit," stated Cassie.

"Give it a chance," said Kyle.

We gave it a chance but it didn't get any better, quite the opposite in fact. There was relief all round when the credits began to roll. We drank some more and listened to Frank Sinatra, Mina singing along under her breath, conducting an invisible orchestra with her finger. I was starting to feel sick. The whizz would be more than welcome.

Cassie yawned and moved to the armchair where Laura was sitting with her legs curled under her. She turned away and finished her drink when Cassie tried to stroke her hair. Since the fight Laura had become pliantly passive when we were fucking, only responding to Mina, and even this amounted to little more than an arching of her back or a finger in her mouth. This didn't really bother me and Cassie had seemed to find it funny, prompting her to call Laura her pillow princess, but now Cassie was frowning, leaning over Laura with her hands on the back of the chair. Laura lit a cigarette with slow care and Kyle asked Bradley how the jeep was running since his tinkering with the engine.

"All right," said Cassie, standing up straight. "You win. I'm sorry. I was wrong to go off without telling you and Mina."

Laura's cigarette froze as she was about to put it between her lips. "And?"

Cassie looked like she was going to throw up. "And it won't happen again," she said.

Laura took a long drag on her cigarette then crushed it in the ashtray. She exhaled a cloud of smoke, watched it dissolve into the air, then she stood up with a smile and kissed Cassie on the mouth, sliding her hand down the back of Cassie's hotpants and pushing her towards the bedroom.

"Is everything back to normal now?" Bradley asked us

when the two girls had gone.

"I think so," said Mina.

Bradley looked relieved. "Wonderful," he said. "The atmosphere was polluting us all. Now we can begin the preparations for Christmas."

Kyle was surprised. "What? Is it soon?"

"Oh yes," said Bradley. "Can't you make out the distant jingling of bells? By the sound of it we're not the only ones who escaped the zeds."

"So it's a trip into town," I said.

"Goody," laughed Mina.

"And no surprises," ordered Bradley. "We all work together on this, it's the safest way."

Boots, trainers, CDs, champagne, superhero T-shirts, movies, piles of make-up, a new football, perfume, books, computer games, a bright pink vibrator, a big painting, silk stockings, candles, an avalanche of clothes, kinky leather masks, ornaments, a retro ashtray, coats, a dartboard, a smoky mirror, a PVC catsuit, a bizarre sculpture, an eye-popping array of underwear, a light sabre, diamonds, rubies, emeralds, comics, wooden fish, a concrete cat, necklaces, ear rings, bracelets, ankle bracelets, belly bracelets, sexy Santa outfits, a machine gun, watches, hats, a vicious knife and an eternity of shoes.

Early on Wednesday morning the seven of us were sitting around the park that was spread across the hill outside Hemdale Gardens. Chloe had driven us here and was waiting inside the warmth of the jeep. Bradley, whose cold was getting worse all the time, was perched on top of the slide in a huge coat. We were surrounded by a small field that had been transforming itself into a jungle before winter came to spoil the fun. The dull view from the hill rippled with houses and roads, the distant cars reflecting the sun that shone brilliantly above our heads.

Kyle was stalking through the grass with the sword in his hands, keeping away the zeds. He'd sliced eight already. He was grinning and talking to himself. There was no shortage of zeds in sight but they weren't grouping and most were labouring up the hill so I thought we'd have plenty of time before having to beat a retreat. Kyle was approaching another zed, a man in what had once been a short-sleeved shirt and muddy trousers. The zed had its head cocked to one side and kept stumbling over the ground. With a grunt Kyle whipped the sword and the zed's left arm fell off. Another grunt and the right had gone too. The zed gnashed its teeth but didn't take its eyes off Kyle. He spun and slashed and the zed went down.

There was a whine of protesting metal that turned into a scream. Laura and Mina were running in wide circles, pushing the rickety steeple of the witch's hat. When it was spinning fast enough they jumped on, standing up and hanging out so that their hair whipped out like streamers. I was sitting on a bench with my arm around Cassie, relying on Bradley and Kyle to spot any zeds that could creep up on us. Bradley sneezed again and blew his nose.

Our Christmas presents were waiting to be wrapped back at the house. No one was looking forward to the chore, which was why we were here in the park. We'd do the wrapping tonight, maybe tomorrow. Our adventure in the City had taken up the whole of Tuesday. We'd chosen our presents spontaneously, keeping well clear of the areas where the zeds congregated. We'd still had plenty of shooting to do, and one or two close calls that could have so easily turned into disaster. At the time it was always so terrifying but once you were back in the jeep and driving away the encounters with the zeds just seemed like a scary movie you'd been watching.

"What was your last Christmas like?" I asked Cassie.

"Not so good," she said. "I had a stinking hangover and I'd dumped my boyfriend on Christmas Eve. He came banging on the door, shouting through the letterbox, he was such a prick. My mother got the baseball bat from upstairs and opened the door. He went away then but he came back with some of his asshole friends later in the night. They threw a brick through my bedroom window."

The girls had finished with the witch's hat and were walking groggily towards us. Kyle had found another zed, a woman this time, pretty too. Kyle sliced off most of her clothes to put her wounds on show. I looked away when he started chopping her up. Laura was beaming as she plopped down next to Cassie. Mina went behind the bench and put her hands around my neck, strangling me and making choking noises. I saw that Kyle was now busy gathering all the heads he'd lopped off. There were eleven of them in all. He carried them by the hair, making a pile on the rubber matting that surrounded the swings. When he was ready Kyle arranged the heads into a circle with all the dead faces looking in towards the centre.

Kyle seemed to steady himself then he stepped into the circle and dropped to his knees. I noticed that the girls were making a show of looking in another direction. Bradley was watching with as much interest as I was. After a few seconds of meditation Kyle took off his coat and tossed it out of the circle. He did the same with his shirt, despite the single figure temperature. I shivered to myself and put my hands in my pockets. Kyle's tan had faded and his skin was prickling with goosebumps. Still on his knees, Kyle held out his arms in a welcoming gesture then clapped his hands together with a loud smack. Holding this position he took slow breaths and closed his eyes. He began talking to himself again. It finally occurred to me that he was praying. I looked at Bradley and he shrugged, wiping his nose.

The seven of us had been together for over a month before we accepted that this was it, our number wasn't going to grow, no one was coming to rescue us and nothing was going to change. It was just us and the zeds. Chloe had constructed her lab a couple of weeks before and the supply of whizz that was snowing us in made our situation a lot easier to cope with. Bradley excepted, the drug fitted us into the zed world where killing and dealing with it were the essentials of life. Whizz didn't give us time to think. It allowed us to act, and to live with our actions.

Cassie's and Mina's decision to dye their hair was for me the final step. This was a new life, surrounded by horror but beautiful at the centre where Cassie lay naked with open arms on a bed of drugs, sex and guns. It was time to start enjoying ourselves. We found that killing zeds could be fun, as long as you'd taken enough whizz and trusted your friends to watch your back. Five of us began going out for no reason other than to shoot zeds. We made a game of it, seeing who could be first to reach a hundred. Cassie began commenting on the beauty of some of the zeds and wondered aloud what it would be like to fuck one of them. She found out that the male zeds were impotent by putting on a show for them in a supermarket car park. When we came out with our trolley to load up we found Cassie standing naked on the roof of the jeep, one hand on her cunt and the other holding a pistol, shooting the zeds that got too close. A few of the male zeds had their flaccid dicks in their hands, trying to get hard with their mouths hanging open and their zed eyes riveted on Cassie as she posed. She saw us standing there and laughed.

Living in such close quarters it was inevitable that we'd pick up on each other's habits, some strange, others endearing, many annoying. Chloe liked to be precise about whizz; her lines had to be of exact length and thickness.

She sometimes spent up to ten minutes cutting her lines just right before vacuuming them up at great speed.

Mina had a thing about Frank Sinatra. She also liked lollipops that painted your tongue different colours, and doing aerobics in front of the tall mirror in the bedroom. I used to watch her while lying in bed with Cassie, smoking cigarettes as Mina turned Frank up high and worked out to her own reflection, her tongue stained orange or purple or blue.

Kyle tended to boast and told terrible jokes that no one ever laughed at. With Laura he was either overly protective or he ignored her completely. He was the most sadistic of us with the zeds, celebrating the most when Bradley found the swords. Kyle sliced with abandon, making it last as long as he could before finishing the zeds off and laughing.

Cassie enjoyed giving orders and hated being told what to do. She didn't like advice, or being helped with anything. She was brave to the point of idiocy, saying that she'd used up all her fear when the zeds first began to appear. Cassie was Queen in the bedroom, moulding our libidos in her own image, playing a tune to which I danced with Mina, both of us enthralled and enraptured by Cassie's chemistry and charms. She was the most bewitching girl alive.

With Laura it was her feet. She scrubbed them with pumice gel, massaged them with peppermint lotion and sprayed them with tea tree oils before agonising over what pair of boots to cover them with. She often left them bare, decorating her toenails a myriad of colours and clipping on the ankle bracelet that always so beguiled me. Laura's were very pretty feet it's true, but surely no feet were so pretty as to warrant the attention Laura gave to them.

I found Bradley too weird even to talk about.

The period over Christmas and the New Year felt like one gigantic day. Time flowed over whizz, drinks and brief snatches of sleep where I dreamt of failing to solve wave equations and trying to crack unbreakable codes. The only solid memory I retained of Christmas Day was the sight of our zeds dressed in the tiny Santa outfits, laughing at them and fucking them while Mina held a candle, singing Christmas carols in a surprisingly good voice.

New Year's Eve was the same but different, our presents still scattered about the house, Bradley unable to decide where he should stand his new sculpture, the girls arrayed in their finery, glittering with jewels. Kyle told us about a drinking game that could be played with one of our new movies. I was the first to throw up but I recovered quickly after cleaning my teeth and doing a few more lines. We paid another visit to the basement but later I couldn't remember who did what to which zed. Eventually, some time in the evening on New Year's Day, our strength gave out with our kidneys and we crawled moaning to our beds. We closed our eyes, opening them again to wake up ravenous after twenty-five hours of sleep.

The gagging smell of petrol was clouding the air around me. I'd washed six times but it hadn't made much difference. Tomorrow the smell wouldn't be so bad but for now I was stuck with it. My arms and shoulders were stiff from using the sword to keep the zeds at bay while Bradley had siphoned fuel from the dead cars. Using guns with all the petrol around would have been more than a little stupid.

I took another shot of vodka, quarantined in the corner of the living room with Chloe, my fellow petrol head. I'd be sleeping alone in Mina's room tonight. Laura was kneeling at Mina's feet, painting her toenails purple.

176

Cassie was sprawled across the couch with Kyle, her hand resting down the front of her shorts. Most eyes were turned to the TV where a pretty girl in her underwear was running away from a killer cop who'd been brought back from the dead by a nerdy college kid with a grudge.

"Better not smoke those cigarettes," Kyle warned me as I reached for the pack, "you'll blow us all to kingdom come."

"Blow this," I said, tossing a candy cane at him and lighting up.

"Now leave this dry," Laura told Mina, "then we'll see if it needs another coat. Stop waving that thing at me, Kyle, just leave me alone."

Mina wiggled her toes and asked Cassie what her New Year's resolutions were.

"Staying alive and to come every day," answered Cassie.

"Mine is to shave my head and become a monk," said Kyle seriously.

"Monks take a vow of celibacy," pointed out Chloe.

"Well, I won't be that kind of monk, obviously."

"What other kind is there?" asked Laura.

"*This* kind," said Kyle, crossing his arms. "I shall become a Warrior of the Lord. You'll see."

The movie eventually came to a close and I slumped off to bed, stopping for a bottle of water on my way. Mina's room was cold and smelt musty. I'd thought she still slept in here quite often but obviously I'd been wrong. I left the light off and undressed then hopped under the sheets. The room was lit a pallid blue by the moon shining in through the window. I looked at it, listening to the dim voices from the living room then hearing movement in the hallway. Cassie and Laura called out goodnight. I grunted in reply, starting to drift.

"Mina?" I mumbled an unknown time later. I'd been

177

woken up by the closing bedroom door. One of the girls was standing there, moving closer now. It was Chloe, taking off her clothes. She pulled the sheets from the bed then jumped onto the mattress. We rolled together, tasting the petrol on each other's skin, the engine fumes surrounding us as we started fucking, making me think of cylinders and pistons speeding along with us in the darkness.

"It's always raining here," complained Bradley from his place at the armoury table. He was stripping and cleaning our guns, keeping them in working order. I sat opposite him with a glass of beer, still slightly confused about fucking Chloe two days ago. Predictably, she'd largely ignored me since. The stripped bed along the wall was lined with rifles, machine guns and pistols. The table was swamped with mysterious gun parts and cloths, things that looked like pipe cleaners and containers of oil and grease. I watched Bradley's nimble little fingers at work as they disassembled a handgun.

"How come you know how to do this stuff?" I asked him.

"I listen to the voices in my head," said Bradley without looking up. "The voices tell me how to do things. The voices know all."

"Really?"

"No, not really. I have some books on weapon maintenance. *That's* how I know how to do this stuff. You think I'm so smart; all that means is a lust for knowledge and the ability to retain it. I'll have to brush up on agriculture soon. We'll dig a garden next door and build greenhouses. We'll grow vegetables instead of killing them or, in your case, raping them. Do you fancy yourself as a farmer?"

"I've never thought about it."

"Try and warm to the idea, it's not like you have a choice. Don't look so worried. This time next year you'll have clay in your fingers and earth in your blood."

"Can't wait."

"Sulking achieves nothing. Pass me that rifle, please. Thank you. Part of your problem lies in the fact that you're not open to new ideas. Existence, like I've told you before, is a fluid process. We have to keep adapting to survive."

Bradley stopped speaking and looked over my shoulder at whoever was standing in the doorway, his face falling. I turned and saw Kyle standing there with his hands raised, bald as a cueball. I started laughing and came close to spilling my beer. Kyle grinned and nodded his gleaming skull.

"Mina took most of it off with clippers," he told us. "I got a razor and did the rest myself. What do you think? Fucking cool?"

"Words fail me," said Bradley, going back to his work.

"Very cool," I agreed, spluttering. I drank some beer, trying to think of something complimentary to say. "I like the shape of your head," was all I could come up with.

"Thanks," said Kyle nonchalantly, still nodding away. "See you around." He strutted off down the hall.

I turned back to face Bradley. "Is that what you call adapting to survive?"

Bradley coughed, or it could have been a laugh.

"I can't really believe he went through with it," I muttered.

Bradley looked up. "Kyle told you about this beforehand?"

"Yes, very recently. It was his New Year's resolution. Shave his head and become a monk."

"A monk? I suppose that it explains Kyle's spasmodic religious mania. One of us was always going break down

179

mentally. I have to admit, I thought it was going to be you."

I gave Bradley the finger and left to get another beer from the fridge. I headed for the living room where I was surprised to find Laura wriggling on Kyle's lap, kissing him passionately with her dress pulled up, his hands busy in her underwear. Chloe was studiously watching the black and white movie on TV. I sat down next to her and poured my beer as Laura pulled Kyle out of the room, giggling in the way she had when she'd popped a few downers. Kyle had time to turn and waggle his eyebrows at me before he was dragged out of sight.

I looked at Chloe. "So is Kyle a monk now, or what?"

"That's very sensitive, Alex," she said. "Thank you."

I felt my face go red and tried to hide it by drinking more beer but I only succeeded in spilling some of the fucking stuff over my T-shirt. Chloe was looking at me and smirking. "Come here," she said.

"What's going on?" demanded Cassie, striding into the room with Mina behind her. "Where the fuck is Laura?"

Chloe closed her eyes for a second then walked out. She opened her bedroom door, said something to Kyle then stomped up to the attic. I wiped the beer off my T-shirt and put the glass back on the table. Mina put a haughty expression on her face and picked her way across the room, hips swinging in a cruel and accurate impression of Chloe. Mina sat by me with her nose in the air. She went to kiss me then drew away, taking a cigarette from the pack. She lit it pretentiously, blew a little puff of smoke in my face and said in a funny voice, "My life is unbearable."

When we'd all finished laughing I told Cassie about Laura and Kyle. She went away to see for herself. Mina gave me the cigarette she'd lit and drank some of my beer,

180

telling me about shaving Kyle's head.

"Let's go," called Cassie from the hall. "I asked Laura if she wanted to come but she's distracted right now. Move it."

We checked in at the armoury where Bradley was still at work. "Careful, children," he said as we selected our weapons. "It grows dark quickly. You won't have more than," Bradley checked his Kingpin watch, "two hours at best. Have fun."

"We will," I chorused with Mina.

Before leaving I finished my beer and we snorted a couple of lines each to sharpen us up. We put our jackets on and off we went, sniffing our way out of the house. I was carrying two pistols like I'd seen people do in the movies. Cassie and Mina had an Uzi each. As soon as the gate shut behind us a zed was moving in. I shot it in the neck, then through the forehead. The zed thumped onto the road. Light clouds were speeding across the sky in the bitter wind. To me it looked like it was getting dark already but I didn't say anything about it. Cassie was tying her hair back to stop it blowing in her face.

We ran down the street, turning the first corner with the wind pushing our backs. Before we grew tired it began raining again, bringing Mina to a squealing halt. We climbed over the nearest wall and trotted up to a squat, ugly house that had its front door hanging open. We went inside and I slammed the door shut behind us. The hallway was mushy and damp, not a friendly place at all. The living room was better, low and wide, everything coated in fine dust. A huge painting of a stag drinking from a pool was hanging above the fireplace.

"That's horrible," said Mina, nodding at the picture.

"We're not here to criticise the art," scolded Cassie, checking her gun. "We'll start through here. I'll go first."

There weren't any zeds in the place and we didn't find

anything interesting until we reached the last room. It was a study, filled with the smell of slowly rotting books. The remains of a man were sprawled across a wide-backed chair. There was a gaping hole in the back of his skull and a revolver was lying on the carpet. What made this really interesting was the camcorder on a tripod that was pointing its lens at the chair. Cassie popped the tape out and held it up for us to see. "Bingo," she said, laughing.

Bradley and Chloe decided to skip the premiere. The rest of us sat in a line across the carpet, fuelled on whizz and gin. We hadn't seen any zeds around as we'd run home through the rain. Maybe the bad weather had kept them away. I didn't know what the situation was between Chloe and Kyle but he seemed happy enough, sitting at the end of the line next to Mina and telling a joke about talking biscuits.

Cassie called for quiet and switched the tape on. The TV screen flickered before showing us a pretty girl lying in bed. She looked seventeen or eighteen and she obviously had the zed virus. We'd all seen this before. It took a matter of hours before it killed you. First came the weakness and a radical drop in temperature, quickly followed by shivers and the sweats. These things grew progressively worse until the victim began convulsing. Next came unconsciousness, and then death. The skin gradually began to glow. Not long after that, sometimes only minutes, the zed would open its eyes.

We all agreed that the girl had one or two hours left before she passed out. A man appeared on the screen to wipe the sweat from the girl's face. The consensus was that this was the girl's father, and that he was the one we'd seen in the chair. He said something to the girl and she smiled in a feeble way then started to cry. The man held her for a minute then he looked at the camera with a desolate expression before stumbling away out of shot.

The tape cut to a different bedroom. I lit a cigarette and put my arm around Cassie as we watched a boy of around Bradley's age lying like a broken doll on his bed, his shivers much worse than his sister's. He didn't have long to go. It was difficult to tell whether he was conscious or not, personally I didn't think so. The boy convulsed, throwing the sheets off the bed and making a gargling sound. He wasn't sweating so much now.

The next scene showed an attic with a crude wooden floor. Boxes were stashed to the left and right. In the centre of the picture a couch had been pushed against the stone wall. Two zeds were tied to it, the girl and the boy. They were still wearing their pyjamas and were staring implacably at an area behind the camera. The boy had bloodstains around his mouth. The zeds' father moved into view, his left arm in a sling. He approached the zeds and knelt down before them, asking if they remembered who they were. The zeds just looked at him with those burning eyes, not a flicker on their faces. The man grew angry and shouted but it wasn't long before he was sobbing, holding the zeds by their shining hands, imploring them to say something. They didn't, of course.

Now we were watching the man at his desk in the study, his face the definition of despair. He opened a drawer and took out a revolver. We breathed in unison while the man looked around for thirty seconds or so, his eyes passing over the camera like it wasn't there. He shuddered, licked his lips, turned the safety off the gun then blew his brains out all over the wall behind him.

"Fucking hardcore," said Kyle, impressed. The man on the screen was turning grey, his jaw flopped open to show us his tongue. The mess on the wall was beginning to drip. Mina looked shaken. Laura's face was red as she lit a cigarette. Cassie turned off the tape, clapped her hands and suggested more whizz.

Much later, before dawn the next morning, I was standing in the doorway of the living room, watching Laura. She'd taken off her clothes and was watching the tape with the lights off, her body lit by the television. One hand was working at her cunt, the other rested on the remote. Laura's hand went faster as the moment of truth approached. She gasped when the gun went off and opened her legs wider. After she came she rewound the tape and pressed Play again.

I walked into the room and pushed Laura onto the floor. Without turning to see who it was she stuck her ass out and opened her cunt with her hand, glistening in the semi-darkness. I fucked her as the tape went on, watching Laura's ass as she fingered her clit, whispering things to herself. She rewound the tape and played it one more time before stopping it and turning to face me. Laura quickly wrapped her lips around my dick, swirling her tongue, her hair tickling my stomach. She made a growling sound when I came, swallowing fast like Cassie had taught her, sucking me until it hurt and I had to pull away. Laura wiped her lips and switched the TV off. It looked like she'd found her kind of pornography.

Chapter 11

Thanks to all the stimulants lying around boredom was fairly rare in our house, but when it hit, it hit hard. The boredom train stopped at many stations on its way down the line; frustration, loneliness, self-pity, horror, desperation, despair, anger and white-hot rage. There were other stations too but white-hot rage was as far as I'd ever got. It was Tuesday afternoon, raining hard. I'd just boarded the train and was clanking down the track, heading for station number one. This train had to be derailed.

Cassie, Mina and Laura were playing cards, and with a pornographic pack of all things. There was no help there. Bradley was in his bedroom, playing some fucking mindless computer game. He was staring at the monitor with glassy eyes and a slack jaw, no more alive than a zed. When I tried talking with him he asked me if I'd like to join Omega Force Three in its attempt to infiltrate the secret headquarters of the Tarkon Federation. I slammed the door on my way out.

"Eight of clubs!" squeaked Laura from the living room. The girls cackled together like the witches they undoubtedly were. With a jolt I realised that I'd already arrived at station number one; frustration. I didn't have much time. I thumped up the steps into the lab where Chloe the chemist was cooking up some whizz. After one look I saw that she wasn't going to help me. That left Kyle, or Brother Kyle as the bald cunt probably wanted to be known. Grinding my teeth, I headed downstairs.

"Queen of Hearts!" shrieked Mina. There was that

cackling again. Bitches were probably wearing pointy hats by now. No one understood me in this place, there was no one to open your heart to, no one to share with. I blundered into Chloe's room where I found Kyle kneeling naked on the carpet, wanking over the shotgun. I watched, appalled, as Kyle grunted and came over the barrel, rubbing his dick over the metal, squeezing out the last drop.

"I'm consecrating this weapon," Kyle told me. "Henceforth no one else may touch it."

"What?"

Kyle smiled, smearing his come over the gun with his hands. He'd painted tiger stripes on the stock. "This zed world is a world without end," he said. "Me and Judgement here are going to balance the scales a little. It came to me when I was praying in the park. This is my purpose, this is my fucking *life*. My flock is waiting for me. The hour is at hand." Kyle threw the shotgun onto the bed and put his clothes back on, finishing by pulling on a pair of big boots and wrapping himself in a huge gunfighter's coat. He passed a hand over his skull then loaded the shotgun with shells. He put an unopened box of them into his pocket.

"I'm leaving now," said Kyle. "I'll be gone for some time."

"Kyle, this is insane. At least wait for the rain to stop."

"Stand aside, Alex. I have work to do."

"What about food?"

"The Lord will provide."

"I fucking *knew* you were going to say that!"

Kyle hefted the shotgun and I got out of the way. I followed him into the garage where he took his bike and opened the door. Kyle wheeled the bike out into the rain and climbed on, starting it up. He smiled a crazy smile and said, "Life's a fucking beautiful thing, Alex, you know that? Fucking beautiful." I just looked while he gave me a wink, rode down the driveway and out through the gate. He was gone. I listened to the bike buzz away into the distance until the sound disappeared and the only thing left was the rain. I was surprised to notice that my train had been derailed. I was feeling better.

As I made my way back into the house I could see a picture of Kyle riding straight into the City Centre and the river of zeds, intent on bringing them all to salvation. I paused in the hallway, undecided as to who to tell first. There could be no avoiding it, it had to be Chloe. I reluctantly climbed the steps back up to the lab.

"You again?" said Chloe, taking off her white coat and picking up a muddy crystal from the table. She chipped a bit off with her fingernail and popped it in her mouth.

"It's Kyle," I said, unable to stop myself wincing. "He's gone. He rode off just now."

Chloe looked puzzled. "What do you mean?"

I found myself backing away. "He said that he might be gone for a couple of days." I didn't think that this was going well. "He took the shotgun," I added hopefully.

Now Chloe was looking stern. "So you just let him leave? No arguments?"

"He wouldn't listen!"

"Why didn't you tell me?"

"There was no time!"

"Did you offer to go with him?"

"Christ, no."

Chloe drummed her fingers on the table, rolling the whizz crystal in her other hand. Her eyes were fixed on the rocket launcher in the corner. "Tell me exactly what happened," she said, so I explained about what Kyle had told me about scales and his flock and the Lord who would

187

provide, but I left out the bit about Kyle coming over the shotgun. "And what was the last thing that he said before he left?" demanded Chloe.

I thought for a second before remembering. "He said that life was fucking beautiful."

Fucking beautiful or not, life had to go on. We went shopping the next day, Chloe driving us in dead silence. I was the one lucky enough to stay with her by the jeep while the others hit the supermarket. A thin fog lay over the ground around us. We rattled off shots with our rifles, taking down the zeds that drifted out of the mist like ghosts. During a lull in the action I tried saying something but Chloe snapped a hard look at me and I obediently shut up.

It was noodles again for dinner. Just why Mina kept bringing this shit home I didn't know. We talked optimistically about Kyle's chances while we were eating. He knew how to handle the zeds, he was used to the environment, he didn't scare easily, he might even be back tomorrow. Chloe didn't take part in the conversation, she just played with her food and drank a lot of wine.

Next up was another Cagney movie. Mina and Cassie had fallen asleep in front of the fire before the film finished. I was sitting with Laura on the floor. Chloe was in her room. When Bradley left after the movie Laura gave me a searching look. "The other night," she said, "with the video." Laura glanced at the sleeping girls. "Have you told them?"

"No," I said, which was true. It seemed kind of obvious that Laura wouldn't have wanted me to say anything about it.

"Good," breathed Laura. "I'd like it to stay that way. It was just a one-off, you know, like an experiment."

"Don't worry," I said, "I won't blab."

"Do you think it was too weird?"

I shrugged. "Who cares? What does weirdness matter anymore? Just take a look at Kyle."

Laura smiled and took her hair down. It fell about her like a shroud. She crawled over to Cassie and Mina then lay down with her head against Cassie's shoulder and her arm around Mina's waist. Within two minutes she was asleep. Bradley interrupted my watching by poking his head around the door. He had that face on again, the one he wore when he was going to say something I wouldn't like.

"Alex? I'd like a word, please."

I followed Bradley to the library. The place was still as neat as his bedroom was messy. A book on horticulture was lying on the desk. Bradley shut the door behind me and regarded me silently. He was wearing his Black Bolt T-shirt, never a good sign. I looked away uneasily, surprised to notice a yellow cloth and some furniture polish almost hidden next to the empty wastepaper basket. I couldn't imagine Bradley polishing away on his little stepladder, cleaning the bookcases, it was too-

"Will you come with me tonight?" he asked me. "I don't expect to find Kyle but it's possible that we could hear his weapon, or his motorcycle."

I sagged against the bookcase, knowing I'd end up going but determined to put up a fight. "What's the point, Bradley?"

"It would comfort Chloe."

"Ask her to go with you then."

"Alex, I'm asking you."

"Why is that?"

"Some would say that you acted negligently in letting Kyle go so easily. They might also say that this is a path of redemption for you, a path that you'd be a fool not to tread. The path may wind uphill, it may not even come to

189

an end, but the joy lies in the journey, the discovery."

"You've been reading too much about trees, hippy."

"Why must you always argue?" burst out Bradley. I liked him better this way. "The City at night is beautiful! Don't you remember the last time? Were you in great danger? Did you benefit from the experience? Did it move you? Was it thrilling?"

Unfortunately the clouds had drifted away as it grew dark. The sickle moon and the stars lit the streets dimly but effectively. Bradley was leading the way with me following at his shoulder. Mina was holding my hand. She'd insisted on coming when she'd woken up and heard of Bradley's plan. Cassie had laughed and opened a bottle of tequila. Chloe had looked pensive. Laura was still asleep. We'd painted our faces like the last time and dressed in black clothes. Each of us carried silenced pistols with two spare clips. Mina was also carrying the short sword, or *wakizashi* as Bradley had named it. We'd been on the move for ninety minutes so far and we'd seen scores of zeds. The important thing was that none of them had seen us.

The plan was to drift around in areas close to the City Centre, always sticking to places we (meaning Bradley) knew relatively well. If Kyle was riding or shooting within a mile's radius, we should have been able to hear him. I was carrying a hipflask filled with Pepsi in my pocket. Before we left Chloe had solemnly dissolved a big pile of whizz in it, making it fizz impressively. As we headed downhill I opened the flask and took another gulp. Mina poked me with her free hand so I passed the flask over. The road ahead was blocked by five or six crashed cars, three of them overturned. Broken glass crunched under our feet as we walked by. A zed in a dress was lying by a postbox, groaning to itself. Another shone in the middle of the road, heading in our direction. We stopped by a Chinese takeaway and stood still. The zed moved silently past us.

"I'm spooked," whispered Mina as we started walking again.

"Taste the air," enthused Bradley, "feel the silence that surrounds us. To be alive amidst this! Isn't it wonderful?"

"Wonderful," I echoed hollowly.

We followed the road as it flattened out and curved to the left. A zed was moaning from somewhere but we couldn't see it. Mina drank more of the spiked Pepsi and swallowed loudly. She burped, the sound like a gunshot in the darkness. The cars were everywhere now, choking the road and forcing us onto the pavement. There was more broken glass around, and a few police cars. We found an army truck that was blocking a junction. There were bullet cases scattered over the ground. Several bodies with cavernous head wounds were lying across the cars or in the gutter. They were practically skeletons now, mossy and grinning at us, watches rusting on their wrists, rings on their fingers.

"I need something to kill," I hissed, the whizz coming on strong. "This tension's fucking me up."

"No killing unless there's no other option," said Bradley softly. "You know how quickly situations can change. If we stood still at this moment and started firing, even with the silencers there would be crowds of zeds here within two minutes. What would you do then?"

I saw Bradley's point and took the flask back off Mina, drinking a little before putting it back in my pocket. After the junction the road widened considerably. We walked down the centre between the traffic, blank buildings rising on either side of us, places that used to sell carpets, electrical goods and toys. Some zeds were gliding around in the car park. I shivered at the sound of their wails. Then a white hand grabbed my fucking ankle and down I went, hitting the road with a clatter. A crawler had me, lurking in-between the cars. It bit the end of my boot and I gasped as I felt its teeth crushing my toes. Metal flashed and I jerked my foot away. The zed's head was still attached to my boot. The decapitated body clawed the ground for a second as if in frustration. Mina wiped the blade and Bradley helped me to my feet. I kicked the head away and it rolled under a car.

"We have to go," said Bradley, interrupting me thanking Mina. "Take a look over there."

The car park zeds had heard something and were moving in to investigate. Two of them had already stepped over the little wall and were blundering against the cars, heading our way. I let Mina go and we trotted away, a surreal feeling sinking into me, dissolving my terror like acid. I grinned at my friends and clapped them on their backs.

"You're right," I told Bradley. "To be alive!"

"I hate those crawlers more than anything," said Mina. She was watching the ground very carefully. "Normal zeds are bad enough but the crawlers are just plain *sneaky*. Is there anything worse than a sneaky zed? I don't think so. I like this sword, Bradley. What's it called again? Waki-something. Well it whacked that zed, anyway. Christ, I'm whizzing my brains out. Am I talking too much?"

"Not too much," said Bradley, "just too loudly."

We followed the wide road for another twenty minutes then took a right at a wreck of a petrol station. There had been an explosion here, there were pieces of cars and petrol pumps everywhere. Bradley pointed out the bones of someone's arm. The hand still clutched a pump handle. I drank more of the whizzy Pepsi with Mina. We moved through tatty streets that were dotted with off licences and mini marts, the zeds wandering about mindlessly in threes or fours. Every now and then we saw a larger group, sometimes over thirty zeds, and we had to change direction.

"Shit," I said, "Pepsi's finished." We were standing at a junction next to a pet store. "Why didn't we bring more?"

"Hang on." Mina was staring at the shop across the road, a place called Aquatix. "This is where dad bought his fish! Oscar! And my little shark!"

"Quiet," snapped Bradley. "Listen carefully. Do you hear it?"

We froze and listened hard. There was nothing, other than the wail from the City. I opened my mouth to speak but Bradley shook his head and put a finger to his lips. I copied him and gave Mina a push. She laughed quietly and padded over to the fish shop to peer into the black windows. Then we heard at; a shotgun blast, distant but unmistakable. It was followed by another. I imagined that I heard Kyle's crazy laughter, then there was the sound of a motorbike that quickly faded away.

Mina rushed back up to us. "He's alive!"

"At least for now," said Bradley.

I turned to look behind us and shuddered, all the good things ripped away. The zeds had been creeping again, perfectly silent, grouping together, forty or more not ten metres away. Mina saw and hissed through her teeth, drawing her pistol. This seemed like a good idea so I did the same.

"Stay calm," said Bradley, all confidence. "Don't shoot. We go this way, not too quickly now. Conserve your energy. Keep your focus."

We jogged up the street past Aquatix, single zeds suddenly popping up everywhere; behind cars, out of houses and shadows, all of them with their eyes marking us through the darkness, following in our trail. Bradley had his pistol in his hand now, using it to point directions. My surreal feeling of euphoria was long gone, replaced by our old friend terror, the most reliable emotion where the zeds were concerned. Mina looked like I felt. We kept close behind Bradley in a tight little triangle, the whizz hammering in my head. Bradley led us past some iron bollards and towards what looked like a railway track. There was a footbridge arching over it. We scampered to the bridge and up the metal steps, stopping when we saw two zeds on the other side, slouching like delinquents. Another pushed its way past them and grunted as it came for us. I could hear something clanking up the steps behind me.

We moved forward to meet the zeds, taking one down each, the guns making a sharp spitting sound. Bradley's zed staggered backwards and fell down the steps behind it. The noise it made on its way down made me put my hands to my ears. We ran across the bridge past the two bodies and down the steps where the zed was crumpled with a hole in its head. There were more bollards, another street and more zeds. I had no idea where we were. I took Mina's hand, both of us forcing shaky smiles.

"Everything's going to be all right," said Bradley, his voice steady. "Now we move quickly. The most important thing is to stay close together. If we become separated we'll be in trouble."

Looking around us it seemed to me that we were in enough trouble already. The street ahead was lit by the zed glow, becoming brighter as we drew closer. It was light enough to read the sign on the side of the first house; Greenberg Road. There weren't too many cars around where zeds could hide and the glow was doing a good job of driving back the shadows. The only zeds we had to worry about were the ones we could see. Where the fuck was Kyle when you needed him?

The zeds were grouping, forming a thin wall. I glanced left and right. The news wasn't good. We shot our way through the first zed wave and started to sprint down the street. The zeds around us stayed in singles so they weren't a problem yet. We only shot the ones that stood directly in our path. This street was a long one and already Bradley was flagging. He could have done with some of the spiked Pepsi that we'd guzzled down earlier. I tried shooting another zed but my gun was empty. I ducked the zed's liquid swipe and attempted to reload but it wasn't easy, not with running and watching for zeds at the same time. Then Mina was gone, grabbed by another crawler, nothing there from the waist down. Bradley shot it and I managed to reload. We got going again, my arm wrapped around the panting Mina's waist. She wasn't moving so well, it looked like her right knee. Bradley ejected an empty clip and slapped a new one into his pistol.

"We should go to ground," I said to Bradley as we ran.

"Suicide," he said.

I shot a zed but only hit it in the shoulder. "But Mina's…"

"It's getting better," she insisted. "I'm running it off."

We'd reached halfway down the street and we weren't going to get any further. The zeds were gathering in front of us, a huge group that was all too close and getting closer. The situation behind was similar, there'd be no going back. We'd stopped running and now waited on the road, sucking in the air with our hands on our knees. The zeds had stopped moaning. The only sound they made was a relentless shuffle.

"This is going to be funky," Mina said with a smile. "How much time do we have?"

"About thirty seconds," I guessed. "Do we save the

last bullet for ourselves, or what?"

"Fuck, no," said Mina. We both laughed and shot more zeds. As we laughed again and kissed, the zeds kept moving in. This was it. Mina's eyes were sparkling.

"You two are so fatalistic," scolded Bradley, typically spoiling the moment. "Can't you see our way out? Follow me."

It was so fucking obvious that I practically slapped my forehead as Bradley led us into one of the houses with the open front doors. He pulled a torch from his coat and switched it on, lighting our way through a short hallway and into the living room. The kitchen was next, then the back door. We found ourselves in a tiny garden surrounded by flimsy fencing. We kicked it down and shot our way into the back of the next house. Bradley killed a zed that was waiting for us in the kitchen. We ran through the hall, this one was longer, then opened the front door and emerged in a new street, a street that looked free of zeds. I was shaking my head in bewilderment as we stepped onto the road.

"You've saved us again," I told Bradley.

"It wasn't exactly difficult," he said crossly.

I watched Mina skipping down the white line and I laughed, shaking Bradley by his scrawny shoulders. "We're alive! Fucking alive!"

"That's true," conceded Bradley. "We also know that Kyle is alive, or at least he was when we heard him. This means that we can go home now. Are you ready?"

Only Chloe was awake when we reached the house. Laura was in bed, Cassie lay unconscious on the couch with the bottle of tequila empty on the floor. We told Chloe the news then washed the paint off our faces and changed back into our usual clothes. Bradley got himself some water then retreated to his room. I carried Cassie to bed as Mina told Chloe exactly what had happened. On the way to the bedroom Cassie opened one red eye and smiled.

"Made it," she said. I shouldered the door open and tipped her onto the bed next to the lump in the blankets that was Laura. I kissed Cassie's cheek then headed back for the living room.

It was only just past midnight and I was exhausted. We snorted a few lines and listened to Frank, drinking gin and running over the events of the night. Back when we were trapped on Greenberg Road I thought I'd felt ready for what was waiting. Fear had heightened through terror to exultation, everything focused on the precise moment, the pistol in my hand, Mina's lips on mine, the closing horde of zeds. Mina had felt it too. Bradley, intent only on escape, had seemed dim, far away.

Mina was looking at me from her place on the chair. Without a word we headed for her bedroom, losing our clothes as we went. We fucked in the darkness as hard as we could, shedding what we'd grown in the City, becoming smaller. When it was done and I was bleeding in half a dozen places Mina turned over onto her stomach and folded her arms beneath her head. I stroked the cooling skin of her back and listened to Chloe cry in the living room.

The house was quiet early on Wednesday afternoon. The only regular sound was the slap of the cards on the table. I was playing poker with Cassie and Chloe, though thankfully we weren't using the pornographic pack. I'd lost a hundred and ten thousand so far. Chloe was the big winner, her face like stone behind her piles of cash. Every so often I heard the bleep of Bradley's computer from his room. Cassie dealt the cards and Chloe lit a cigarette. What did this tell me about the hand she had? I tried vainly to recall Chloe's cigarette habits during the game so far then I was interrupted by the sound of a motorbike.

Our eyes widened simultaneously. The money flew everywhere as we jumped to our feet and ran to the front door. Chloe threw it open and we tumbled out onto the driveway. The gate was sliding open. In rode Kyle, new shades over his eyes and grinning like a maniac. He got off his bike and left it on its stand. It wasn't the same bike he'd ridden away on. Kyle's hair had grown considerably. He took off his shades, putting them into his coat.

"Judgement and I have ridden far and wide," he announced, "spreading the Word of the Lord."

"Don't be such a twat," said Cassie. "Where the fuck have you been?"

"Walking with Jesus," laughed Kyle, "but now I'm back, home where I truly belong. Looking good, Alex. What do you say, Chloe?"

Chloe approached Kyle and slapped him very hard across his face. He didn't even blink, he just smiled wider as Chloe hugged him then pulled away, making a face. "You stink like a polecat. Get in there and wash."

We interrogated Kyle all day but he only came back with the same cryptic crap he'd given us before. In the end Chloe had lost patience and stormed up to the attic. In response Kyle cracked open a bottle of bourbon and handed it around. Mina told the story about our adventure in the City. Kyle laughed long when she came to the part about hearing his shotgun and his bike. We finished the bourbon and started another bottle.

"You know," said Kyle benevolently, putting an arm around Laura and kissing her cheek, "I missed you all when I was gone, even you, Brad. No, don't speak. I know you feel the same fucking way, we all do. Maybe next time I won't be away for so long. A toast! To the Children of God! Long may we serve Him!"

After downing his glass Kyle threw it over his

shoulder and went to search for Chloe. I was trying to work out whether it felt good to have Kyle back or not. The issue was a tricky one. Bradley, looking like he'd just sucked on a lemon, crawled to the video and put Casablanca on. When he was crying over the final scene I still hadn't resolved the matter so I gave up thinking about it and stole glances at Laura's ankle bracelet instead.

"That fish place made me think," Mina said, her head on Cassie's lap. "I want to see my old house again. I want to see my room."

"Easy," said Cassie. "We'll go tomorrow."

Mina smiled and yawned. "Don't any of you want to see home?"

"Not me," said Cassie.

"Nor me," said Laura.

"This is home," I said, thinking of my brother Tim. That fucker.

Bradley wiped his eyes and blew his nose. "I agree with Alex. The past may send itself to the present but I don't think it has to arrive."

I woke up in an uncomfortable tangle of limbs. That was Kyle's arm. This was Laura's leg. I prised myself out of bed and pulled on some new clothes. I found Cassie in the kitchen, drinking coffee in her bathrobe with a towel wrapped around her hair. She didn't say good morning. Instead she said, "Did you and Laura really fuck Kyle last night?"

"That's right."

"But he's acting like a complete cunt!"

"So what?" I said, pouring water into the kettle. "He's still Kyle."

"I'm not so sure," said Cassie. "I don't know if I can trust him anymore."

"You'll find out this afternoon. He's coming with us

199

to Mina's house. So is Chloe."

"One big happy family," Cassie said, taking the towel from her hair and shaking it out.

Mina's house was still easy to spot due to the ragged remains piled outside it. There were no moving zeds to be seen. Chloe parked the jeep and we stepped out onto the road, breathing in the silence, checking our weapons, checking for zeds. Chloe and Kyle were going to remain with the jeep. The rest of us approached the unremarkable house, Mina in the lead. She fished for a moment in her jacket pocket and brought out a key attached to a rubber eyeball, twirling it around her finger.

The front door was stiff but with a bit of shoving we managed to get it open. The place smelt rank. We were standing in a tiny hallway, stairs climbing in front of us, rooms to the left and right. We went right first, the dining room and short corridor of a kitchen. Dirty water had pooled around the back door. Mina picked up a mug that had a cartoon lion on it. She smiled to herself then tossed it into the sink. Laura was checking her reflection in the dusty mirror. I could see Chloe watching our shapes through the window.

The fishtank that Mina had told me about was in the living room. The tank was long and deep but the water was so cloudy that I couldn't see anything inside. Mina tapped her nails on the tank, ignoring the rest of the room. She shook her head and led us upstairs, past the bathroom and to her bedroom, the one with the purple door. The bed was unmade, the dresser choked with clutter. The blue bin in the corner was full of crisp packets and chocolate wrappers. Three curling photographs of a scowling boy were stuck onto the tall mirror.

"This is where I first saw you," Mina said to Cassie, both of them standing at the window. Three plates and a bottle of lemonade were at Cassie's feet. She put her arms around Mina and kissed her neck. Bradley was looking critically at the books lined along the shelves above the bed. Laura was looking even more critically inside the wardrobe, alternately raising her eyebrows and wrinkling her nose. I joined the girls at the window and saw Kyle waving at us in a jolly kind of way from the street below. He pointed the shotgun at the window and I flinched backwards. Kyle laughed and said something to Chloe.

"This house is as dead as the others," said Mina in a cracked voice. "There's nothing left anymore. I want to go now."

I asked Mina if she wanted to take anything with her. She turned to face the room, casting her eyes around. She moved to the dresser and opened the bottom drawer while Laura continued her inspection of the wardrobe. Mina pawed around then took out a photograph. She handed it to me then left the room. Cassie peered over my shoulder with her bubblegum breath as we looked at the photo of Mina, taken a couple of years ago. Her hair was very short and she was gazing with wonder and delight at the fishtank downstairs, eyes rapt on the little black shark that was swimming towards her face.

"That's a good one," said Cassie. She chewed thoughtfully then blew a pink bubble that popped in my ear.

Chapter 12

Laura was watching the tape again, hand in her underwear. This time I waited until she'd finished before going into the room. Laura tidied up her dress and looked at me, only slightly red faced, as I sat down next to her. She took the gin and tonic I was offering. It was early on Monday evening, just beginning to get dark. Bradley and Chloe were in the lab. Cassie and Mina were in bed. I didn't want to know where Kyle was, or what he was doing. Laura stretched like a cat and lit a cigarette. "Our little secret," she whispered in my ear, then she kissed me.

"Just don't let Bradley catch you," I warned. "He'd lecture you until you bleed."

"To death," laughed Laura. It was her birthday tomorrow. We'd gathered presents from the City last Friday, the usual collection of clothes, jewels and trinkets. And boots. This morning Mina and Cassie had gone outside on an errand. They wouldn't tell me where they were going but it had to be something to do with tomorrow's big occasion. I'd been bluntly warned by Cassie not to breathe a word of my suspicions to Laura.

"I'm tired," she said, lying back and putting her legs over mine. "I could do with a hit."

"There's nothing left," I murmured, running my hand over Laura's smooth skin, smelling peppermint lotion, stopping at her ankle bracelet and trying to circle it with my hand. "What did you find in Mina's wardrobe?"

"A lion and a witch," said Laura distantly. "Don't tickle me."

We both jumped when Kyle suddenly began to bellow

'Onward Christian Soldiers' from the bedroom. What his voice lacked in harmony was made up for what it had in volume. Before Kyle could finish the first verse we heard someone storming through the hallway and into Chloe's room.

"*Kyle!*" yelled Cassie. "*Shut the fuck up!* Thank you. Now take your hands off your dick and put some fucking clothes on."

Laura giggled as Cassie went back to her room. It wasn't long before Kyle walked in wearing jogging trousers and flip-flops, swinging a bottle of bourbon in his hand. He sat on the floor and took a glum shot from the bottle. I eyed him warily. Four or five shots later Kyle was looking much brighter, he even apologised for making such a racket.

"What's happened to you?" Laura asked him. "Why are you acting like this?"

Kyle drank some more, leaning his head back against the wall. "It isn't easy to make you see," he said, "but God holds me in the Hollow of His Hand."

This hangover was the worst ever, a living hell. I thought it was Wednesday morning. I realised that I was retching and that I was lying on the floor. I opened my eyes to face a sticky pool of bile. This was the dining room. All the chairs had been tossed into the corners and the table had been overturned. Six empty champagne bottles and a feather boa were lying around me. It had been Laura's birthday, that much was clear. I tried to remember more but the effort felt like glass shattering in my head, making me retch some more. Remembering would come later. First I had to get cleaned up, then I had to find some clothes. Locating one of the others would be helpful too.

While I was crawling for the living room I realised

that I was missing something obvious, something to do with my skin. There, on my hand. Blood. It was on the other one as well. A lot of blood. *My* blood? I had to stop so I could check my body. When I turned over and saw the gore that was covering me I passed out without a whimper.

It wasn't my blood. I was crawling for the living room again. Someone was groaning in there, a girl. Luckily the door was open. I crawled on through and saw Cassie, Laura and Mina lying in a pile on the floor, all breathing, naked, looking like they'd taken a shower in a slaughterhouse. The stink was unbelievable. Cassie was the one who was groaning. I checked her first. She threw up as I turned her over. No injuries, just blood and what seemed to be bits of internal organs. Mina was next. It was the same story. Laura was the messiest out of all of us. Her hair was like a bad red dye job, matted from end to end. She was wearing a little leather mask over her eyes. I tried to get if off but it was stuck to her skin. The other door opened and Kyle came staggering in, as fucked up as the rest of us, holding a piece of paper. He dropped to his knees, crumpling the paper and grabbing my arm. The girls were starting to move. Laura turned and vomited. There was even blood in the mess that was coming from her mouth.

"The note," said Kyle, his breath reeking, "from Bradley. He's gone with Chloe. They'll be back in two days, when the fuck is that? What's it today? The note says we should clean the place up before they come back and that if we don't know what happened we should check the tape in the video."

"Fuck that," I said. "I need a wash." I was cut off by Mina, who'd seen the mess and started screaming.

Everyone was ready before midnight. We didn't feel clean but at least we looked it. The blood and the vomit in the living room were taken care of. That still left the dining room, the kitchen and the hallway. We'd fix that tomorrow. I'd checked the cellar with Cassie. The place was pristine, as were our zeds. I thought that if I tried hard enough I'd be able to remember what happened but I just wasn't keen on the idea. The video would be easier.

Like the last time, we were sitting in a line across the carpet. I was between Laura and Mina, all of us drinking the tea I'd made, Cassie and Laura smoking cigarettes. I lit one as well. No one was worried about Bradley and Chloe. They'd have found a safe place long before now, probably not far away. Cassie was holding the remote. She pressed a button and off we went.

There was Laura, opening her presents and laughing, making a point of not looking at the camera. After the presents were opened the scene cut to Laura in a new dress and boots, the pink feather boa around her neck. The rest of us ran into the shot, apart from Bradley who was holding the camera. We popped the champagne and opened the vodka, the tequila and the gin. Chloe was sorting out the whizz. Drinks were drunk, laughs laughed and whizz snorted. We sang Happy Birthday and Laura blushed.

Next up Laura was doing the tango with Cassie, the dance looking good, at least to me. More drinks, more whizz, more drinks again. Mina was behind the camera now. She filmed Bradley going to bed, following him down the hall until he ducked into his room and shut the door. The picture on the screen weaved its way back to the living room where Laura was gulping tequila from the bottle. I was trying to kiss Chloe but she was pushing me away. Cassie and Kyle were mixing drinks in tall glasses; champagne, vodka and gin.

We were all shouting in the next scene. I couldn't hear what we were saying because the music was too loud.

Chloe was looking angry. Eventually she strode out of the room and slammed the door. We all cheered, then vacuumed up more ragged lines. Laura picked up one of the brimming tall glasses and got to her feet, the feather boa slipping off her shoulder and falling to the floor. Laura composed herself then tipped the evil drink down her throat, spilling some over her face. When the glass was empty Laura dropped it and staggered over to Cassie, grabbing her hips. I was sharing one of the other tall glasses with Kyle. Mina dropped the camera to join in the fun and then the only thing we could see was an extreme close-up of the carpet.

Now we were watching Mina belt out a Frank Sinatra song to Laura, who was busy kissing Cassie. Kyle was pouring whizz into five glasses of champagne, which meant that I was the one who was holding the camera. I put it down clumsily on a chair and our headless bodies drained our glasses, which were so fizzy that most of it went up our noses, causing mass laughing fits. The scene cut to a close-up of a thick line of whizz that had been cut across Mina's hips and shaven cunt. Laura snorted it, doing a good job of licking up the residue. Cassie cut a new line, then it was my turn, then Kyle's, then Cassie's. Mina snorted hers over the curve of Cassie's ass.

We were staggering naked down the hallway, falling over nothing with bottles in our hands. Laura was wearing the little black mask. Cassie stopped outside the spare bedroom and leaned against the wall. She called Laura over and put an arm around her waist, whispering to her. Laura giggled and drank more gin from her bottle. Cassie kicked the door open and pushed Laura inside. We all heard her squeal of delight before piling in the room ourselves.

The only light came in from the hallway and from the glowing zed that was tied to the mattress on the floor. It was the girl in the tape whose father blew his brains out. She must have still been in the attic, waiting for Mina and Cassie to pick her up. The zed was blonde, gagged and beautiful. Mina attached the camera to a tripod as Cassie started lighting the candles that were scattered around the room. Laura finished her gin and threw the bottle aside. She swayed to herself for a few seconds while Cassie finished lighting the candles. Someone closed the bedroom door. The light was murky but perfectly adequate, the zed the moonlight centrepiece.

Over the next hour we watched ourselves fucking the zed in every we could think of, always drinking more vodka and tequila, the whizz we'd taken the only thing keeping us conscious. By now we were crawling around the floor with hollow eyes and slack jaws, going back to the zed again and again for another taste of her icy soft skin. Someone brought the whizz from the living room and we finished it off, washing it down with the last of the alcohol.

Laura was standing up with her hands on her head. She started a snaky dance and ran her fingers over her mask. The rest of us were kneeling around the zed, looking up blankly at Laura as the whizz took effect once more.

"I'm here," said Laura, "I've arrived, oh fuck." She giggled spookily and fell to her knees on the zed like she was worshipping it. The zed convulsed as Laura whipped her head around, digging her face into the zed's side. Laura came up with a chunk of flesh in her mouth and zed blood began to spill. Laura spat it out and dipped her finger into the zed's wound. It came out bloody up to the knuckle. Slowly Laura sucked her finger clean, eyes closed. She opened them and smiled with bloody teeth.

We fell in a howling frenzy on the writhing zed, laying her open with our hands and teeth, the zed's glow burning fiercer every second. When we pulled back we all had bloody faces and wide eyes. The zed on the mattress was thrashing with her insides on show, her heart motionless in her chest. We were all panting heavily, watching Laura take down her hair. She brought it forward, dipping it deep into the zed and running her fingers through it until all traces of blonde were gone and it was washed in gore. Laura tossed her head, slicking back her new red hair then thrusting her hands back into the zed, squeezing what she found there. She pulled her hands out and started to finger herself, smearing her cunt with blood, her other hand leaving a messy trail up over her stomach, her tits, reaching for her hair, pulling it until she came.

While the rest of us got back to work on the zed Laura stood up and slinked towards the camera, flicking her hand and spattering blood on the lens. She kissed the glass then looked at us behind her mask and through the red print of her lips that she'd left on the screen. Laura was smiling at us as she turned the camera off, the screen breaking up into interference.

I didn't know what I should be feeling. The zed would have to be cleaned out of the spare bedroom. Messy job. I welcomed the shadow of nausea that fell on me as Cassie switched the television off. Mina had covered her face with her hands, shrugging off Cassie's questioning touch. Kyle seemed vaguely puzzled about the whole thing. Laura was glowing pink, her eyes distant. I could see how this had upset Bradley and Chloe. What were we going to say to them about it? Would we pretend it hadn't happened?

"Let's pretend it never happened," I suggested, lying in bed but not wanting to sleep yet. The longer tomorrow could be delayed the better.

"Sounds good," said Mina hopefully.

"Sounds stupid," said Cassie. "It *did* happen. We had a great time."

"We let go," said Laura. "It was beautiful."

I fell asleep not long after that. With the morning came the clean-up. We opened all the windows and got to work, leaving the spare bedroom until last, which when we walked in didn't look beautiful to me. Kyle cleaned with great gusto, working twice as hard as the rest of us. He was head of operations in the final room, the stink apparently not touching him at all. Under his directions the room was as clean as it was ever going to get just before noon. We all piled the refuse and the remains of the zed in the back garden next door. Kyle poured some petrol on and struck a match. None of the girls waited to watch the fire, preferring to go back to bed. I stayed with Kyle. When the zed was starting to crackle I asked him how he felt about what we'd done.

"Communion," he stated simply.

"Isn't that blasphemous?"

"The blasphemy is what surrounds us, the zeds. Nothing else comes close."

We waited silently with the fire until the sound of a jeep's engine began to grow. Then we trudged to the front of the house and out onto the street. I was carrying a pistol, Kyle had nothing. We opened our gate as the jeep was pulling up. Chloe drove past us and up the driveway without a glance in our direction. Kyle followed me inside and we closed the gate behind us.

The first snow of the year was a disappointment. I watched it fall limply from a dismal sky through the window in Bradley's library. He was at the desk scrutinising a book about postcards or something. It had been six days since we'd ripped up the zed. Laura still hadn't got all the blood out of her hair, it was driving her crazy. Chloe had been frostier than usual but she hadn't said anything about the zed, at least not to me. The snow was already turning back into sleet. I turned away from the window and spun Bradley around on his chair. He didn't look up from his book so I spun the chair some more then left for the living room.

Yesterday five of us had ridden out in search of zeds. We stopped at a swimming pool car park, spacious but isolated, plenty of zeds about but not enough to swamp us. We purged ourselves with the machine guns then switched to the baseball bat and the swords. Cassie took a few Polaroids, Kyle did his thing with the circle of severed heads, taking his top off and praying in the centre. I had one tricky moment with two big, messy zeds who seemed impervious to the bat, but Cassie shot them both before they could fall on me.

Kyle was lying flat out on the living room carpet with Cassie straddling him, performing one of her famous massages. Kyle was groaning but powerless, his legs kicking weakly. Mina was studying the photograph of herself and the shark. I'd fitted it into a frame that I'd found while rooting through the drawers in the kitchen. I flopped down next to Mina and Cassie told Kyle to stop fighting. "Resistance is useless," she added. Mina's expression didn't look sad as she stared at the photo but tears were coursing down her face and splashing onto her arm. Laura was sprawled like liquid over the couch. She was wearing bracelets around her wrist, her stomach and her ankle. She looked at me and waggled her foot, smiling lazily. Someone had put classical music on the stereo, probably Mina. I wiped a tear from her cheek and tasted it. Salty. I couldn't remember how the zed had tasted but I knew it wasn't like this. Were we all cannibals now? As well as murderers? Rapists? What the fuck did it matter?

"You're killing me," whined Kyle. "Let me up."

"Not until I'm done," said Cassie. "I can't believe you're so tense, especially here, and here. Must be all that praying you've been doing."

"It's so distant," whispered Mina, eyes still locked on the photo. She started to cry harder and I put an useless arm around her. Then I had a better idea and reached for the bowl of downers on the coffee table. I popped two pills into Mina's mouth and handed her some water. Cassie continued to pound Kyle's back until she was satisfied that he'd suffered enough. She released him but Kyle didn't move, he just groaned some more and complained that he was paralysed.

"Tomorrow you'll be a new man," smiled Cassie, pleased with herself. She pushed her way into the middle of the couch, taking the tiara off her head and putting it on Mina's to cheer her up. "That haircut was a big mistake," Cassie said, looking at the younger Mina in the photo.

"I know," said Mina, sniffing. "I did it to piss off my mother. It worked good."

"I still can't move," said Kyle.

We were at a pharmacy this time, opposite a post office and flanked by solicitor's offices and estate agents. It was an icy afternoon, piercingly bright. Chloe was still wearing the shades she'd had to put on to drive. The zeds, all looking different, all exactly the same, were moving in across the road, out of doors and broken windows. We stood firm around the jeep, picking the zeds off, putting them down. Maybe it was just the whizz talking but there appeared to be an underlying thread running through all of this, a connection. It began with our fear, for ourselves and our friends, fear of the enemy and the joy in their destruction. Yet the zeds were legion and fearless with it. Who could know what it was like to be a zed? Perhaps they welcomed our bullets, pushing each other to be first in line for oblivion, yearning for release. Maybe Kyle was right, and we *were* the zeds' saviours.

This led the thread back to ourselves again. I tried to shake these useless thoughts off and to concentrate what I was doing. I shot another five zeds then had to reload my rifle. The girls would be coming out of the pharmacy soon. Reloaded and back on track, I raised my gun and got back to work. Zeds fell down and were trodden on by others who fell down themselves, were trodden on by others again, the repetition near and far, played out until the girls returned and we plunged into the jeep, leaving the scene behind.

"There's a thread," I made the mistake of saying, immediately drawing the attention of Bradley sitting next to me.

"What do you mean?" he asked wide-eyed.

"Well," I began, not knowing what I meant anymore, "this thread, it joins us to the zeds, you know, it brings us together, like it was all meant to be, like we need each other."

Bradley continued with the wide-eyed look.

"You're thinking too much," advised Kyle from the front seat. "Place your trust in the Lord. He'll guide you with His Sure fucking Hand, see if He doesn't. It works for me."

"Shit," hissed Laura, running fingers through her hair. She picked another clot of zed blood from a pigtail, opened the window and threw it outside. "I'll be doing this forever," she said.

"The time is coming once again," announced Kyle. "I'll be riding out tomorrow morning. I'm sorry, Chloe, but I have no choice about this. My fate is not my own. I won't be gone for too long this time."

"You can be gone forty days and forty nights for all I care," said Chloe, making Cassie laugh, then something

212

went wrong with the jeep, everything went shaky and Chloe said, "Puncture."

We all started talking at once before Bradley banged the roof hard with his fist. "Chloe, turn into that street on the right, stop after ten metres. Kyle and Alex are with me, the rest of you kill all the zeds you can. We mustn't give them time to mass. Kyle, you detach the wheel. I'll take care of the jack. You'll have the spare wheel, Alex, you should be able to empathise with it. That's far enough, Chloe. It's time."

Out we went, not too many zeds around. The girls started shooting as we rushed to fetch the tools and the wheel. I'd never done this before and my shaky equilibrium was further eroded with every shot that was fired. The puncture was at the front on the left hand side. Bradley was having trouble with the jack. My guess was he'd never done this before either. Cassie was the closest of the girls, machine gun in her hands. Bradley finally got the jack to work and started pumping away at the handle. The jeep was rising inch by inch. I felt naked without any weapons on me.

"I can't raise it any higher," panted Bradley. "Alex, take over."

So now it was me who was pumping the handle and Bradley standing ready with the spare wheel. Kyle was looking around at the street and smiling wistfully. The shots were coming quicker all the time. At last the jeep was high enough and Kyle got to work on the hubcap then the wheel, giving me time to see what was going on with the zeds. Most of them were scattered behind us, coming from the road we'd just been driving along, but there were more than enough gathering in front as well.

Kyle was straining with all his might but as yet he hadn't moved a thing. For some reason Cassie had stopped firing. Her fucking gun had jammed. Bradley helped Kyle as I ran with Cassie into the jeep. She grabbed the Uzis and I took a pistol. We moved back into position but the zeds had taken their chance and were moving in fast. This was getting ridiculous.

"Hurry up!" shouted Laura from behind us.

Cassie opened up with the Uzis and I got off a few badly aimed shots with the pistol. The zeds started falling again. Chloe stopped firing to reload her rifle. By now Bradley and Kyle had loosened two of the nuts on the punctured wheel. I emptied the pistol into the zeds then tossed the gun back into the jeep. Bradley raised his head to check on the zed situation then he jumped to his feet and began to speak but I couldn't hear him over the gunfire.

"*Abort!*" he screamed at us. "*Abort!* Get the weapons and go!"

Experience had taught me to listen to Bradley so as Kyle began to argue I swept an armful of guns from the jeep and laid them on the road. There were more in the back seat so I added them as well, and some spare ammunition. The girls were too busy shooting to know what was going on. Bradley picked up the last remaining machine gun with its one spare clip and joined Laura and Mina at the back. Kyle took his shotgun and a box of shells. I slung a rifle over my back and grabbed two pistols, one of them empty. Kyle moved next to Chloe as I loaded the empty gun. Now the only things left on the road was a magazine for an Uzi and two for the rifles. I stuffed them in my pockets and hurried to Cassie.

"Fucking hell!" she yelled. "What's happening?"

Before I could answer Bradley had appeared with Laura and Mina in tow. With the seven of us shooting as one the zeds folded before us. Bradley moved forward and Cassie shook him angrily by the shoulder. In answer he pointed behind us so I turned to see a tide of zeds, six of

214

them already crawling over our jeep. The situation was clearly fucked up. We ran up the street, leaving our ride behind.

This wasn't like a walk around friendly Hemdale Gardens. We were much closer to the City Centre and we'd already been shooting for the last few minutes, the sound bringing in the zeds from all directions. What we needed was a car we could use as a getaway vehicle, the quicker the better. Luckily for us cars weren't exactly in short supply. We stopped at the first one that wasn't blocked in or smashed up. No keys. I asked Bradley if he knew anything about hot-wiring.

"Of course I don't," he snapped as we carried on running.

"What happens if we don't find a car we can use?" gasped Mina.

"Then we die!" said Kyle happily.

"Shut up," said Cassie, taking down two more grasping zeds. "Let's try this one."

Chloe heaved the door open and slid into the front seat, fucking zeds everywhere. I could have jumped for joy as I heard the jingle of keys. The car wouldn't start. "Shit," said Chloe, trying again, but it was obvious that the car's problem was terminal, just like our problem if we didn't get moving soon. Chloe climbed out and we moved on, blasting our way through the street until we reached the next available car, which wouldn't start either. Same story with the next one.

"Change of plan," said Bradley. "I think we'll have more luck with a car that hasn't been standing on the street for the last ten months. We need to find a garage."

"Look around us!" cried Laura. "Nothing but houses! What are we going to do?"

"We're going to keep our heads," said Bradley. "This isn't as bad as it seems. We move to the next street, and

215

don't waste any bullets. What's the most important thing, Alex?"

"Stick close together," I answered, stupidly pleased for remembering this.

"Right," agreed Bradley, killing three zeds.

"A bad fucking day," Cassie said as we got moving again.

The next street was the same as the last, only it had more zeds on it. We cleared a way through and headed down a side street but as we turned the corner we were confronted by a solid zed wall. The zeds herded us back the way we came until we were trapped on the road. The gunfire began once more as I remembered what had happened the last time we were in a situation like this. I started checking the houses around us for open doors that could provide escape routes. There was one, but a zed was staggering out of it. There was another, two doors down.

Zeds were closing in from every direction, there was no time for a fucking committee meeting so I grabbed the hand nearest to mine, which was Mina's, and I pointed to the open door. The zeds were on us now so I ran with Mina and the others behind me. Crawlers were pulling themselves out from beneath cars, snatching at our ankles as we jumped and weaved and shot our way into the welcoming house. Then I saw what had happened. The only people following me were Mina and Chloe. The others had gone with Bradley to a house on the opposite side of the street. There was Cassie, yelling at us from the doorway. Mina started out from our house to meet her but Chloe pulled her back. We looked at Cassie over the zed road until Bradley pulled her inside and shut the door. Chloe slammed our door closed and we stood in the dim hallway as the zeds started scratching outside.

"We haven't got time to cry," said Chloe, glancing nervously down the hall as I stared at Mina as she was staring at me. Chloe shook us, spilling tears from our eyes.

"We'll find a car, we'll find a car and pick them up. Can you hear me? We have to go."

Mina pressed cool lips to my forehead and I tasted another of her tears from her cheek. Windows were breaking from somewhere too close. Zeds were tumbling inside. Chloe led the way through the house and out into the back. The walls around the garden were high and old. I boosted Mina up, then Chloe. The girls dangled their hands down to help me scramble up myself. I made it just as the zeds were spilling out of the back door.

We dropped down into a jungle alleyway, all puddles and potholes. There had to be a garage here. We hurried past broken walls and rotting sheds. Mina stopped when she heard Kyle's shotgun and a machine gun burst. Was that a scream? I pulled Mina on, no breath in my lungs, and Chloe called out, waving us forward. This was what we'd been looking for; a double garage recently built, shattered security lights perched on top. I nearly failed to notice the zed that was approaching from nine o'clock. I put a bullet in its head while Chloe worked on the garage door. After a few well judged shots she managed to force the door upwards.

A jeep was waiting for us, smaller and sportier than our old one but it would do nicely. First we needed the keys. Mina opened the door in the back and told Chloe to wait with the jeep. I followed Mina through the garden to the house. Mina blew the door open and we stepped inside. The keys were hanging on a tacky rack that had been screwed to the wall. Someone a long time ago had been interrupted doing the washing-up. There were dishes in the sink and broken crockery over the floor, scattered across the bloodstains. Mina took the keys from the rack, looked at me with a haunted face, then bent over the table and pulled down her tracksuit bottoms. "For luck," she told

217

me. After fumbling with my jeans I pushed my cock into her, holding it there with my hand on Mina's hard stomach. She whispered Cassie's name, then Laura's. I pulled out and we tidied ourselves up before running back to the garage.

Chloe changed the oil and the battery in the jeep before she said that we could go but at last we were on our way, through the alley and out onto the road, past the zeds and onto the street where Cassie and the others would have emerged. Sure enough there were zed bodies littering the road along with bullet cases and shotgun shells. There was no sign of movement though, other than the zeds.

The next street told us nothing new so Chloe began pressing the horn, the horrible blaring drawing even more zeds and tying our tension up into ever more intricate knots. The massing zeds made it impossible for us to stay in one place. We drove around the streets making as much noise as we could, looking for any sign that the others had been here, doubling back when it was possible, the pressure of Mina's hand on my shoulder increasing by the minute until the door of a car we were approaching opened and Laura burst into view with blood on her face. Chloe stopped the jeep and I got out with Mina. Laura hit us like a bullet, rocking us back against the jeep. Mina bundled Laura inside and I shot the zeds that were getting too close.

Laura found it difficult to speak at first but she soon overcame it and told us what had happened, her hands clenched in Mina's. It looked like the four of them had passed through two houses and into the next street where there were more zeds than ever. Cassie had wanted to go back but Bradley disagreed, backed up by Kyle. Cassie hadn't listened of course, she'd run off with Laura not far behind. As soon as Cassie had passed the front door a zed had fallen on her, then a crawler took hold of Laura,

218

bringing her down. Bradley had shot it, splashing the blood over Laura's face, then Laura grew incoherent, there were too many zeds, she didn't know what was happening, she was screaming for Cassie, there was more gunfire and some shouting before Laura opened the car door and hid inside. She'd heard us pass once before but there'd been too many zeds around for her to show herself. Laura pulled her hands out of Mina's and took one of my pistols. Chloe turned the jeep around.

This was the house where Cassie had run into the zed. The door was still open. I felt nothing but a numbing cold as I led the way inside. There was no body, no zed. Cassie's guns were lying on the carpet. Something was banging upstairs. Then I was shoved aside and Laura was running up the steps with Mina behind her. I followed and saw Laura struggling with a messy zed, trying to find a headshot. Mina put the zed down, attracting the attention of five more zeds that were clawing at a closed door. Another moved in from the bedroom. After our gunfire stopped and the zeds were dead a girl's voice cried out.

"You took your fucking time!" it said. "Those cunts were nearly in! Wait, I can't open the fucking door!"

We cleared away the corpses, laughing at the battered door, splintered and bloody from the zeds' attacks. We kicked it down and Cassie leapt out into our arms. We danced around the fading zeds, cackling and kissing, telling snatches of our stories until Chloe blasted the horn outside where we found more zeds to kill before driving away to search for Bradley and Kyle.

Over the next hour we found a trail of zed corpses that led slowly but surely to an alleyway that looked weirdly similar to the one where we'd found the new jeep, except that this alley contained more garages, all of them forced open, the last one decorated with a huge cross that had been painted on the wall in red paint. Did this mean that we should check this house as well? Chloe thought so, but the search turned up nothing. No one had been inside since the zeds came.

My mood was sinking fast as I sat in front with Chloe on the way home, listening to the girls chatter behind us, thinking about Bradley. Was he alive when Kyle painted that cross? Was the cross some kind of memorial? That seemed like something Kyle would do. No, Bradley was alive. He was our brain, just as Cassie was our heart. I glanced over at Chloe, who was driving with a grim expression as we passed the sign that led us into Hemdale Gardens. Then a motorbike roared out of a driveway and shot inches past the front of the jeep, Kyle riding with his top off, howling with laughter and Bradley clinging on behind him, white faced and terrified with his eyes screwed shut.

"This lunatic's even more dangerous than the zeds," Bradley told me when we met outside the house. "He could have killed me in seven entirely separate ways."

"The Lord protects me," said Kyle happily, whacking Bradley on the shoulder then bellowing, "The Lord protects us all! Long is His Arm! Blessed His Name!"

Chloe was shaking her head as she led the way into the house. "This was such a stupid day. So much went so wrong."

"But we made it," laughed Mina.

"Then let's celebrate!" said Cassie, holding Laura and Mina by their hair. "Bring me whizz and gin!"

So the lines went up and the drinks went down as we told our stories once again while Bradley took solace in his library. We played football in the garden until it grew dark then five of us took a trip into the basement and played with our zeds until we could stand their cold no more. Then it was time to pop some pills and sink into the furniture, losing ourselves in music and finally crawling our way into bed where we fell on Laura like zeds under water.

"*Fuck me,*" Laura whispered to us, "*fuck me till I die.*"